Aisl .. ya Rai & Other Stories

WINNERS OF THE COMMONWEALTH SHORT STORY PRIZE 2024

Aishwarya Rai & Other Stories

WINNERS OF THE COMMONWEALTH
SHORT STORY PRIZE 2024

The Commonwealth Short Story Prize is administered by the

Commonwealth Foundation. You can find out more about their work at:

www.commonwealthfoundation.com

Aishwarya Rai & Other Stories:
Winners of the Commonwealth Short Story Prize 2024

This edition has been published in 2024
in the United Kingdom by Paper + Ink.

www.paperand.ink
Twitter: @paper_andink
Instagram: paper_and.ink

1 2 3 4 5 6 7 8 9 10

ISBN 9781911475682

A CIP catalogue record for this book is available from the British Library.
Jacket design by James Nunn: www.jamesnunn.co.uk | @Gnunkse
Printed and bound in Great Britain.

CONTENTS

CONTENTS

ABOUT THE COMMONWEALTH SHORT STORY PRIZE

The Commonwealth Short Story Prize (CSSP) is administered by the Commonwealth Foundation. Now in its twelfth year, the prize is awarded for the best piece of unpublished short fiction (2,000 – 5,000 words) from any of the fifty-six countries of the Commonwealth. Regional winners receive GBP 2,500, and the overall winner receives GBP 5,000. The most accessible and international of all writing competitions, it is free to enter and open to all Commonwealth citizens; entries can be submitted in English, Bengali, Chinese, French, Greek, Malay, Maltese, Portuguese, Samoan, Swahili, Tamil and Turkish, as well as the Creole languages of the Commonwealth. Entries can also be submitted as English translations from any language. The international panel of judges selects one winner from each of the five Commonwealth regions – Africa; Asia; Canada and Europe; the Caribbean; and the Pacific – one of which is chosen as the overall winner.

CSSP 2024 Judging Panel
Chair: Jennifer Nansubuga Makumbi
Africa: Keletso Mopai
Asia: O Thiam Chin
Canada and Europe: Shashi Bhat
The Caribbean: Richard Georges
The Pacific: Melissa Lucashenko

About the Commonwealth Foundation

The Commonwealth Foundation is an intergovernmental organisation established by heads of government in support of the belief that the Commonwealth is as much an association of peoples as it is of governments. The Foundation is the Commonwealth's agency for civil society, which seeks to nurture the growth of vibrant and free societies, championing the active participation of citizens in all aspects of governance. Its cultural programming is founded on the belief that creativity and storytelling can inspire constructive action and bring about positive change in the world. The Foundation works with local and international partners to deliver its cultural projects and platforms, including *adda*, an online magazine of new writing; a pilot Creative Grants scheme launched in 2021; and the prestigious Commonwealth Short Story Prize.

www.commonwealthfoundation.com
www.addastories.org

AISHWARYA RAI

SANJANA THAKUR

The first mother Avni brings home is too clean. She wears white at all times, perpetually a mourner, and roams the two-bed flat with a feather duster tied to her slim wrist. "Don't I look just like Aishwarya Rai?" she asks, and pours bleach into the bathtub and onto her body. *Scrub-a-dub-dub*. Avni asks her no questions and takes her straight back.

At the shelter, they lead her to the back and shoot her. "She's had multiple placements," they explain. "Sometimes, this is the humane option."

The second mother is mean, and very, very beautiful. *This one actually does look like Aishwarya Rai*, Avni thinks. *A star*. She buys a weighing scale and makes Avni stand on it and watch the numbers wobble.

"Too high!" she decides when they steady.

"Let's play a game," Avni says, stepping off the scale. She crosses her arms over her body and watches as she shrinks in the mirror. "Would you rather have a fat, happy daughter, or a daughter who is thin and sad?"

The second mother doesn't hesitate: "Thin."

"And sad."

"Yes," she agrees.

Avni nods. "How do you sleep?"

"Too well," she confesses. "Like a baby."

● ● ●

The shelter people take her back, no problem. She has a highly desirable look, they say, and will find another home quickly. And does Avni want to take another look around?

Avni does.

The third mother is sad. All she talks about is the village she came from, where she'd had cows and babies who all died one by one. She'd longed for a living child her whole life, she says. Avni has never been to a village, nor once felt the urge to milk cows.

"Did you love your husband?" she says, and when the third mother nods, asks

why.

"My choices were to love him or not," the third mother says. "And loving him seemed easier."

"That's a good answer," says Avni, and decides to keep her – at least for a while. They learn each other slowly.

Third Mother wakes each day to make kadak chai and drink it on the two-by-two-foot balcony with a wrought iron railing that Avni never uses except to dry her underwear. Third Mother drinks several cups of chai a day. Third Mother cooks in the late afternoons for dinner and next day's lunch. Third Mother packs tiffins and sends them to Avni's office with the neighbourhood dabbawala. Third Mother puts too much salt in her food, but Avni's tastebuds adjust. Avni starts to crave salt. Avni likes having a hot lunch every day. Avni likes having a hot dinner. Avni likes that Third Mother snores, because she can hear it through their shared wall. Avni has panic attacks when she tries to sleep. Avni gets cold all over and her legs twitch like the limbs of a dying insect. Avni feels frightened and lonely and frequently lightheaded. Avni needs company in the nighttime, but Avni doesn't like men.

"How old are you?" Third Mother asks one week into living together. She's opened the small kitchen window for ventilation while she fries bhindi in hot mustard oil. Through the metal bars, Avni can see the alley, and past it into the balconies of the building next door. In the early mornings they are parrot perches, and in the afternoons, drying racks. In the nights, smoke spots for fathers, sons, rebel daughters.

"Twenty-three," Avni replies. "You?"

"Thirty-seven," she says. The bhindi crackles.

"You look much older," says Avni, surprised. "It must be all the grief."

Third Mother wears salwars on weekdays and sarees on weekends, and tries on short dresses from Avni's cupboard when Avni isn't home. She marks her parting with sindoor and has long, butt-length hair that Avni pulls from between her teeth at mealtimes and out the shower drain each week. Her eyes are deeply lined.

Avni panics on a Saturday night and doesn't know why. Her arms and legs spasm, stop being hers. She clenches her muscles for ten seconds, breathes in, breathes out. She wants to call her mother, but they haven't talked in nearly six months. She folds her knees under herself and leans forward in child's pose. She lets her belly hang between her thighs. She tries to rest her forehead on the floor, but fails. She times her breaths to Third Mother's snores and makes it through the night.

"How did you sleep?" Third Mother asks the next morning, and Avni lies:

"Fine."

Third Mother hums, but doesn't push.

Avni had thought that she liked that about her. She doesn't say anything. She says, "Do you need anything washed?"

Third Mother brings her a basket full of clothes and cotton panties with lace trims.

Avni's bedsheets are soaked in sweat. She strips them and throws everything into the machine. She sits, watches soap bubbles form and froth and go round in circles. The day is a wash. *Scrub-a-dub-dub.*

●　●　●

"Why did you choose me?" Third Mother asks one day while Avni is making coffee.

It has been nearly a month since Avni brought her home. The knobs for the stove stopped working years ago, so Avni turns the dials until she hears the click of the gas, then holds a lighter to the burner until it catches flame.

"You looked like all the mothers on TV," Avni says. All the mothers on TV look tired and sad, like they are single-handedly holding their families together.

●　●　●

At work, Avni adds subtitles to ads for shampoo and Knorr instant-soup mixes. Her desk is infested with roaches, but the view is good. Sixteen floors high, the Arabian Sea a kilometre away. Aishwarya Rai tosses her gorgeous, bouncy hair over her shoulder and says, *Total Repair 5: Because we're worth it.* A little boy says, *Mom, do we eat or drink this?* and his mom replies: *Knorr Soupy Noodles! Swallow how you like.*

The noodles make Avni hungry. She sneaks away. Outside the front of the building, there's a Starbucks and a Suzette; to the back of the building, under big swathes of tarpaulin stitched together, a khao gully. She buys a vada pav for thirty rupees and asks for extra salt, extra chillies, extra bhajji. Her mother had never let her eat street food growing up. She breaks off small bits of the soft, buttered bread and feeds them to the calico on the corner.

Her job bores her. The cat accepts crumbs from her hand then sets to work with her rough tongue. *Scrub-a-dub-dub.* All detergent ads are the same. A child comes home from school dripping in mud; a mother says, *Ay-hay!* But she isn't angry. She knows she can fix this. Avni remembers this from her own childhood. Laundry's an easy thing to fix.

Her mother calls. She doesn't pick up, and feels guilty about it. She doesn't want to fight.

They'd fought frequently when she was young: about Avni's weight, and her face, and her body, and her birth. They were very good at fighting – they always said things that were mean and true. Avni would say something mean and true, like, "You're just a mother", and Mother would say something meaner and truer, like, "I was going to leave your father but I got pregnant with you." Then Avni would run away to the terrace and pretend that Aishwarya Rai was her real mother, that any minute she'd show up in a white stretch limousine and take her away.

Avni strokes the cat's white patches. The cat blinks at her, and she blinks back. She'd heard that slow-blinking is a way of saying "I love you". When the cat wanders away, she goes back upstairs. Dating apps. Wellness drinks. Travel agents. Paint. Bridal lehengas. Coffee. Gold. Food delivery. Dabbawala delivery. Third Mother sent mooli ke parathe and thecha. The parathe are soft and flaky. The thecha is sour and spicy and tingles the inside walls of her mouth. Her coworkers buy food from the trolley like she used to, but she finds it bland now. Lacking salt.

She cries on the bus home. There's the salt. She licks her stinging lips and thinks of Mother.

"Tell me about her," Third Mother says, when Avni explains why she's been crying.

"She was a size four her whole life," Avni says, "except when she was pregnant with me, and then she was a size eight. She was a bad cook, but a good baker. She never let me lick the spoon. Her Victoria sponge was so soft, you hardly had to chew. She didn't love my father until she had me – and then she had two choices, and loving him was easier. She loved yoga; she could carry her whole body on the palms of her hands like a crow. She didn't have any friends except me. I was her only friend. She thought Saif Ali Khan's voice was sexy. And she sang to me most nights."

"She sounds nice," Third Mother says. They hug for the first time. Third Mother's arms circle her shoulders loosely, cautiously. Avni finds it lacking.

In the morning they brush their teeth side by side, *spit-spit-gargle-spit*. The Colgate is minty-fresh and the shower is freshly wet and the bathroom smells like mehndi. They drink chai on the balcony, then Avni drives Third Mother back to the shelter.

In the car she whites and wilts and asks what she has done wrong. Avni notices, newly, the way her hair catches a copper tang under sunlight, like Aishwarya Rai in 2008. She doesn't know what to say.

The shelter people fuss over Third Mother and give each other knowing looks. "Perhaps," they suggest gently, "you might try an older mother? One with more training and experience?"

The shelter houses one hundred and fifty women who used to be or long to be or have no choice but to be Mothers. They live in small double rooms with identical furniture. They cook together in a common kitchen and grow tulsi plants on the windowsill. On Sundays they sit in a long line that winds its way past the rooms and around all the living-room furniture. They oil and braid each other's hair. Avni did high school community service hours here. They seem happy enough to her.

"All right," she decides. "I'll give it a shot."

They bring out a tall, unsmiling woman with white hair pinned behind her ears. "Avni," they say. "This is Nazneen."

* * *

And so Nazneen becomes the fourth mother. She is significantly older than the other mothers. Practically a grandmother. She is stern, but when Avni drives them home she rolls her window down and sticks her head out to feel the breeze. Then she laughs and laughs like a child.

Nazneen makes different food than Third Mother had done. Lots of meat, cheap cuts … but perfectly cooked so as to fall off the bone. She is from Hyderabad, and buys whole chickens straight from the butcher. She makes Avni learn how to clean and cut.

"It's gross and sad," Avni says. "I don't want to do it."

"If you want to eat, you will cook," Nazneen replies, unfazed. "You have got yourself a mother, not a maid." She places the chicken on a wooden chopping board. "See," she says, indicating where with her big knife. "If you can, always cut through the joints instead of the bones."

Avni watches as she makes clean lines across the body of the chicken until it is disassembled. What's left looks less like bird and more like meat.

"This knife is not sharp enough," Nazneen observes. "Got it?"

Avni nods. Her mother calls, and she hits IGNORE.

Nazneen's face softens. She cuts breasts, thighs, drumsticks, wings into small, fairly even pieces. "This is called karahi cut," she says. "Your mother never taught you?"

"No," Avni says. "She must have thought other things were more important."

"Like what?"

Avni shrugs. "I don't know," she says, picking up a piece of raw chicken and squishing it between her fingers.

Nazneen thwacks her hand with the hilt of the knife, and she puts it back down. Nazneen says, "Tell me more."

"There's nothing to tell," Avni says, pressing her damp, sticky fingers together. "My mother never really cared for food. And I think I was a disappointing child."

She was not a beautiful child. The last time she had spoken to her mother, she had been on her knees. They were doing yoga together in her mother's spare room. Child's pose. Avni couldn't fold herself forward far enough for her forehead to touch the floor then, either. Her stomach got in the way. Mother had been genuinely sad. She had said, "You look nothing like me."

The chicken karahi has less salt than Avni is now used to, but it's moist and delicate and she hardly has to chew. She swallows; Nazneen pretends not to see her tears. It goes down easy, and there's the salt.

They do dishes before bed. Avni scrubs, Nazneen rinses.

Nazneen doesn't snore, so Avni feels extra-alone in the nights. She can't sleep again. She paces the flat and tries to regulate her breathing. Over and over, she counts down. *Five things she can see, four things she can feel, three things she can hear, two things she can smell, one thing she can taste.* She watches people smoking from the kitchen window. She chews ice; she throws away the weighing scale.

"I heard you," Nazneen says in the morning. "Do you often sleep badly?" "Yes," Avni says, stirring instant coffee into her bubbling milk.

"Does anything help?"

Avni shakes her head. "Nothing you can do."

"Something for another mother, perhaps?" Nazneen guesses.

Avni takes her coffee to go.

●　●　●

At work, she gets to observe a shoot for the first time. She is tired and jittery, and building a booth with thick black cloth in the lobby of an ugly high-rise near Atria Mall. She stands in for the model while the cameramen set up their lights. She moves as instructed. She flinches at the flash. She closes her eyes when the lights get too bright.

"You, move!" someone yells.

When Avni opens her eyes, there – two feet away, surrounded by hair and makeup ladies, dressed in all-white with strings of pearls wrapped around her swanny neck, wind machine blowing her hair dramatically back – is Aishwarya Rai.

The shoot takes hours. Aishwarya turns this way and that, offers long, slow, catlike blinks to the cameras. She is selling VOLUME SHOCKING MASCARA, and it is shocking how beautiful she is. Avni tries to lock eyes, tries to slow-blink back at her.

They break for lunch, and someone brings around chutney-cheese sandwiches for the crew. Aishwarya sits on one of those high makeup chairs and feeds herself a Caesar salad. Avni watches. The pieces of romaine are too big. Oh no. They're smudging her perfect makeup. Her personal assistant is putting on a pair of disposable gloves. Her personal assistant is ripping each romaine leaf into smaller bites, one by one by one.

"Chai?" someone says.

Avni takes it without shifting her gaze. She drinks without shifting her gaze. She spills chai on her white shirt and says, "Shit!"

Aishwarya hears; Aishwarya sees.

Avni doesn't know what to do now that they are actually holding eye contact. She slow-blinks. Aishwarya's eyes narrow, but she does not blink back. From somewhere else in the room, the director claps his hands loudly and Aishwarya disappears under a fluster of people armed with cotton pads and makeup brushes and bobby pins.

Avni dabs at her shirt, but she only makes the stain worse.

Her boss's boss's intern, a skinny man in skinny jeans and a *ganji*, comes up to her and says they don't need her anymore. She can leave.

"But what if I don't want to leave yet," she protests, holding the shirt away from her body and squeezing. A few drops of chai fall to the floor.

"Sorry," he shrugs. "Aishwarya Ma'am wants you gone."

"No," Avni says, letting the fabric go. It falls back onto her body, sticks wetly to her stomach. "Why?"

The intern tugs at his ganji uncomfortably. "She said you scared her?" He says it like a question.

In Avni's head, an image reverses: a white stretch limousine pulls up outside a middle-class apartment building in Panvel, Aishwarya Rai inside. The passenger door opens, then closes. The limo speeds off. A young girl picks herself up off the ground and watches as it disappears.

"Aishwarya," Avni says, as the intern tries to tug her away. "Aishwarya, I'm sorry!"

From the midst of all the makeup artists and hairstylists, a long, pale arm extends outwards and rises up like a kind of deity. It offers a graceful red-carpet wave. *Goodbye.*

Avni drives home in a very regular sized Maruti Suzuki.

When she arrives, Nazneen is at the dining table. She has found Avni's old photo albums and is looking through them carefully.

"Hey," Avni says, reaching for the book. "No."

Nazneen flips, unrepentant. "Is this your mother?" she asks. "It must be. You look just like her."

Avni sucks in a breath. She sits down. "I don't want to talk about her," she says.

Nazneen closes the book. "I do," she says. "Do you want to tell me what's wrong?"

"Not really." Avni gets up and moves to the kitchen. Nazneen follows her in. She takes off her shirt and stands over the sink in her bra. The Vim is running out, she notices. She drips what's left onto the top and turns on the geyser, then the tap. *Scrub-a-dub-dub.* When she bends over she feels her stomach curve and expand over the waistband of her pants.

"Why don't you call her back," Nazneen says.

"I can't let the stain set," she replies.

Nazneen takes off her dupatta and drapes it over Avni's shoulders. She says, "I would like you to take me back to the shelter."

"What," Avni says, dropping the shirt. "Why?"

"You should be using Surf for this. Never mind." Nazneen takes over. She switches off the geyser and turns the tap to the coldest temperature. She soaks the stain. A few minutes pass. She says, "I don't think I am the right mother for you, Avni."

Avni laughs. "What a shit day this is," she says. She pulls the dupatta over her body and covers herself.

"I am sorry to upset you," Nazneen says, switching off the tap and wringing the shirt with all the ferocity of a TurboDry until the excess water has sweated out. "But I don't think you will find what you are looking for in a new mother."

Avni says, "Let me put on a shirt."

❉   ❉   ❉

The shelter people are tired of her; Avni can tell. *What is wrong this time,* they ask, *and why has she returned, and doesn't she understand adoption is a serious lifetime commitment?*

Avni says she is very sorry for troubling them, and lets Nazneen go. Nazneen doesn't try to hug her. She takes her hand and holds it just long enough for Avni's to feel warmed.

"You must have been a good mother," Avni tells her.

Nazneen smiles. "You say that because you are not my daughter."

● ● ●

In the house, Avni finds her white T-shirt drying on the balcony that has been unused since she took Third Mother back to the shelter. It is spotless, as if the stain had never been there. As if the chai had never spilled. Somehow she knows that she could have done exactly what Nazneen did and still made everything worse instead of better. *Something-something mother's touch.*

She goes to bed without eating, and can't sleep. Her stomach feels as though it is being wrung dry and her head is on a spin cycle, being vigorously washed. *Scrub-a-dub-dub.* She draws her legs up to her chest. She clenches her muscles, she breathes in, she unclenches her muscles, she breathes out. She picks up her phone and calls her mother back.

"I didn't call you to fight," she says as soon as Mother picks up.

"I know why you called," Mother says. "I can always tell."

"Sorry," she says, and feels better already.

"You can't do like this," Mother tells her. "Calling me only when you need me."

Avni closes her eyes and decides to say something mean and true just one more time. "If I call you when I hurt," she says, "you make it better. If I call you when I'm not hurting, you make it worse."

Mother says, "Well," and blows her nose loudly.

"Sorry," Avni repeats. The breath at the other end of the line tells her Mother is still there. She pictures her in bed at this hour, in one of those thin cotton nighties she buys from Love Lady every spring. For better or worse, she knows Mother as well as Mother knows her.

"Do you want to hear about my day?" Mother asks finally. "Do you want me to sing for you?"

"Yes," Avni says. Her head slows down. She uncurls her legs slowly and evens out her breathing. She stretches out so her whole body is flat against the mattress. "Please."

And Mother starts to speak, and Mother starts to sing.

DITE

REENA USHA RUNGOO

She collected stamps when she was younger, then switched to books, degrees and – when she moved abroad – white lovers. Later she returned to the familiar, and turned to teas. The careful, deliberate steps of preparing her tea became a habit, and as with most habits, it was folded in with ingredients and histories preceding her.

She bought teas from regular stores and specialty houses, on errands to the local grocer and visits to her home island. Friends indulged her and added to her hodgepodge collection. Once, on her birthday, a lover took her on a surprise trip to the Davenport and Sons tea house, and she came back home with quite the loot. In this way, we grew into uneven rows of boxes and tins on her shelves, a dry garden tended by love and ritual.

Back home on her island, household altars were commonplace, erected in a special room in the house or assembled in a dedicated corner of the living room. Some altars housed statues and images of goddesses, garlanded with flowers. Others held pungent incense and the photographs and personal belongings of dear departed ones. Irreverently, Durga liked to think that her boxes and tins, fragrant and framed by a pell-mell of old teapots and chipped mugs, were her altar.

Then she gave us up. We know exactly when it happened.

It was when Durga came back from Dadi's funeral in Mauritius. Her grandmother's passing had emptied her heart of home, even as her travel bags were heavy with the familiar foods of her childhood. Sifting through them, she carefully removed a sealed envelope and an unassuming blue box labelled BOIS CHÉRI VANILLA TEA. She placed both at the back of the shelves, behind the rest of us, hidden from view. She threw out the food. And then, as if the newcomers had tainted us with their presence, she avoided us for a long while. Almost a decade elapsed as we gathered dust and waited patiently.

Then Mama left the island and moved in with Durga, to the island in Massachusetts. The day she arrived, she dug out the blue box from behind the lot of us and proceeded to make tea in the same manner she had done every day of her life back in Mauritius. She flavoured it with cardamom pods, crushed lemongrass roots and the Red Cow milk powder she had brought with her. A simple family recipe. The familiar hustle and bustle drew Durga to the kitchen. Mama had made her a cup without asking, which soothed and irked her in equal measure. She brought the cup to her lips and inhaled.

Durga had moved from island to island, up socially and away from familiarity, discarding everything except for her journals – and us. She started writing as a teenager, and kept the habit well into adulthood. Her journals recorded her life *(les filles à l'école ont remarqué mes chaussures Nike, ça valait la peine d'avoir*

économisé mon argent de poche toute l'année;
Rajiv m'a souri, je pense que je suis amoureuse;
Durga – – , PhD!). And so did we. But the
carefully constructed narratives, which Durga
wrote in impeccable French and interspersed
with exciting milestones, were not for us. Our
domain is smells and associations, the quotidian
and the transient. As we punctuate frantic
mornings and lazy afternoons day after day, we
modestly gather, in aromatic interstices between
our leaves, the quiet intimacies of humans.
We are no different from a beloved fruit from
childhood, an old wooden toy or the last song
on a mixtape, lost and found again. We are easily
forgotten. That is, until we remember.

As Durga inhaled the tea her mother had made
her, its aroma bloomed into a remembrance as
intense and engulfing as it was evanescent. A
childhood memory, which had coalesced around
the long-buried but instantly familiar fragrance
of the tea, invaded her nostrils. Her body at
once retracted and protracted into prepubescent
angles, all knees and elbows. As the tea burned
her throat, she was recalled into the body she

used to inhabit, and the ways in which it had inhabited the world.

* * *

Bring water, loose leaf tea, five cardamom pods and one crushed lemongrass root to boil in a small deksi. Add three teaspoons of milk powder, mix well and remove from heat.

* * *

The kitchen is small and warm, the loud, flower-patterned curtains are open and the tropical afternoon sunlight floods in through the window behind Mama. The smells of our old house in Riambel float around: fried fish, garlic and thyme, milk and cardamom, salt from the sea breeze. I do not yet know where one ends and another starts. I will unfurl and catalogue them to make sense of the tangled threads of a lost archive, long after I have left my island.

I am back from school, ravenous. Usually, Mama makes pudinn vermisel for teatime.

Today I smell gato franse. Like all the women in the neighbourhood, she borrows on credit throughout the month from boutikier sinwa, the grocer who keeps tabs in a large, tattered notebook: rice, oil, flour and, when we start going to school, exercise books and pencils. Like most of the men, Papa drinks on credit from the local bar. At the beginning of every month, his pay is swallowed by the previous month. But occasionally, when there is still some money left, Mama buys gato franse like feuilleté custard, napolitaine, maspain – those local pastries with French names that are uniquely Mauritian and for which Muslim bakers on the island seem to have a special talent.

As she hands me tea and a napolitaine, I cannot quite see my mother for the light behind her, and I pray that she does not see the red shape imprinted on my cheek. Like all children at Permal Teeroovengadum Primary School, I know better than to tell my parents.

The teachers each have their own style, moulded by calculated sadism, dogmatic righteousness or blinding anger. They also have their own tools, hewn from dried bamboo culms, coconut fibre rods or badamier stems. I sometimes imagine the Permal Teeroovengadum Primary School teachers taking a walk with their families on weekends and stopping in their tracks when they find just the right cane, as if waiting to be stripped of its leaves and polished.

When I am eight years old, in Standard 3, the lashes begin. I have been coddled enough the first two years of primary school, I am told. Monsieur Hassan's cane, which he hides in a different place every time, appears out of nowhere and provides a swift lash for mistaking the French acute accent for the circumflex, or confusing Grande Rivière Sud-Est with Grande Rivière Nord-Ouest. No matter that we know the local names of our rivers, their depths and swells, like our own backyard. The cane disappears just as quickly as it appears. By the time the pain comes, the punishment has already ended and relief has taken over. Monsieur Hassan then makes a slightly clownish face as if to mitigate our humiliation, or maybe his own discomfort towards what he believes he must do. He is the nicest of the twelve schoolteachers.

Guru Manikam is not our teacher but often visits, unannounced, to chat with Monsieur Hassan. His enormous handlebar moustache twitches as his big red eyes scan the class. Once, they pause on Ahmad, who freezes. Guru Manikam beckons, and Ahmad walks to the front of the class, eyes wide with silent terror. Guru hooks his index finger around Ahmad's waistband, pulls it toward himself, and peers inside. He murmurs thoughtfully, as if deciding on which fish to pick at the market, or debating the merits of a particular rédaction. We collectively breathe a sigh of relief at not being Ahmad. Monsieur Hassan makes a clownish face and looks away.

The following year, Madame Ramsarai teaches Standard 4. She specialises in shaming rituals. When Preeti and Sarah-Anne, whom she forces to sit in the back and well away from everyone else, start chatting instead of following the lesson, she calls them to the front of the classroom. She pulls a chair close to her own desk, as if setting a stage. She sits Preeti in the chair, parts her hair gingerly with a pen, and shows Sarah-Anne the lice and nits. Sarah-Anne picks them between her index finger and thumb and quickly crushes them between her fingernails. They make a satisfying pop, and it makes Sarah-Anne smile. This goes on for a good half-hour until it is her turn to sit and get her hair cleaned by Preeti. The rest of us look over to the spectacle from time to time, but mostly we carry on with our rédaction.

Madame knows that we do not quite fear her the same way we do her male colleagues, and she gets creative. Once, she tells us to wear our best uniforms, clean and ironed, for a dictée the following day. A dictée is a special occasion after all, she says. And don't forget to wear your best underwear, she adds, as we laugh. The next day, she calls to the front of the classroom all those who have omitted their silent *t*'s and *d*'s or have spelled *-aux* as *-o*. Their backs facing the rest of the class, the boys are asked to pull their pants down, and the girls to lift their skirts, before the obligatory lash on the buttocks for each mistake.

At the end of primary school, every child on the island competes in a national exam, and Monsieur Beekoo is our teacher for the last two years. His reputation precedes him. Out of the thousands who take the exam, his students regularly rank among the first five hundred, going on to join so-called star secondary schools. The rest go to regular schools, vocational schools or no school at all. Monsieur has a panoply of punishments in his arsenal, and they flow out of frustration for the avoidable mistakes his favourites make – and indifferent disregard for the rest. When he asks me to conjugate the verb "instruire" in the perfect tense, my tongue betrays me, skips over the pointed French *u* and flattens directly into the *i* so familiar in my native Creole. I feel the sting of the slap after he starts yelling, his face inches away from my own.

Like the teachers, the pupils each have their own style. Some jump and yelp, their eyes widening in surprise at every lash, their eyebrows disappearing into their hair. Others overdo the crying, hoping to soften the teacher's heart, although we all know it never does. And then there are those who attempt to flee the lashes altogether, but with one arm in the teacher's vice-like grip they only manage to dance in a revolving circle. I stand tall and silent, holding in my cries until my throat hurts more than the welts on my body.

I will soon leave for the Catholic secondary school Monsieur Beekoo and Mama wish for me. There will be no lashings there. It is, after all, a star school, one of the most respected. There we will mostly just suffer detention, either for wearing short skirts (Rule 7 from the Code of Conduct: the hem of the skirt needs to be at or below the knees and not reveal too much skin) or for speaking in Creole (Rule 2: only French allowed). Sometimes, when we fail to remember the main themes of Proust's *Du côté de chez Swann*, a blackboard eraser is thrown in our general direction, easily dodged. And in my case, a teacher will replace my surname daily with funny ones from Voltaire's *Candide* when doing roll call. I will stand tall and silent through it all, feeling no pain at all except for the strange one in my throat.

Presently Mama notices the red marks on my cheek, the ones left by Monsieur Beekoo. She promises not to tell Papa, but sits with me at night while I write lines: I conjugate "instruire" in the present, perfect and future tenses, and copy each ten times. I do not need my Bescherelle conjugation book. My written French is excellent, as Monsieur Beekoo himself tells me. When Mama gets up and starts to make tea for both of us, she tells me that I am lucky to be in school. She tells me that I need to focus and get an education, so I won't be at my husband's mercy one day. Or so I won't end up even worse, like our neighbour: raising her daughters on her own, working night shifts in a tea factory where women are vulgar and curse in Creole – just like the men.

* * *

Bring water, tulsi leaves and ginger slices to a boil. Remove from heat and strain. Add this water to your own waters, for the sake of your unborn child.

* * *

Water is primordial memory. My first memory, like my first water, is not my own, but Mama's. It is of a time before I am born, stitched together from the bits and pieces my aunts share with me, weaved into my sense of self, the prologue to my story.

In this sepia-coloured memory, I imagine Mama to be very thin, not showing yet. The additional weight from carrying and birthing three daughters will come later. As will the calluses and cuts on her hands from cleaning and cooking: washing bedsheets and cloth diapers, grinding ginger, garlic and masala with the small, rounded baby rock on the tall mama rock outside. When Papa yells, he says, bour to sime ale – get the fuck out. They have always rented, never owned, but he says, this is my house. When he yells, Mama thinks of her last day in school, the day before she turned fourteen. School was not free in pre-independence Mauritius, and her brothers were a better investment. She stayed at home to look after them, and to clean and to cook, wash clothes and grind spices. When Papa yells, to enn fam lakaz, you are a housewife, you do not work, she thinks of how she has had to work for men her whole life. But she does not say anything.

In my borrowed memory, she has one foot out the door of his rented house, as if about to leave. But she does not. Instead, she drinks the tulsi and ginger brew standing squarely in the doorway, putting all her hope in her unborn child.

I see all of this as if watching from outside that house in Riambel, hiding behind the hibiscus tree like a thief. The light in the house floods out of the doorway where Mama stands, and she is all chiaroscuro. I mostly see her movements in silhouette, but I imagine her standing tall and silent, drinking in her tea.

When I am pregnant, Mama will make me a brew with tulsi leaves and ginger, and tell me that when she was pregnant, she used to stand in the doorway and drink the same concoction. Old women said that if she did this, her son would be tall. You don't have any sons, I will say back. And

Mama will laugh, as she often will after leaving the rented house and moving in with me. Me mo bann tifi edike, she will respond after a moment of reflection, giving in to my defiance. But my daughters are educated. And she will tell me that I am a professor of French because of her, that I am the tallest woman of the family because of her.

* * *

Pour hot water over a tea sachet and let steep for five minutes. Add warm milk. Enjoy with a cucumber sandwich or scone.

* * *

I find a table at Quill and Ivy, the only tearoom on campus. A few students around me are having tea and sandwiches, some of them working on their laptops or reading. Vandana, the only other Mauritian student I know at the university, works there part-time. She hands me a tea sachet in a handsome black-and-gold sleeve, next to a small creamer full of warm milk. The sleeve reads VANILLA COMOROS. The vanilla bean, which gourmets associate with Bourbon (now Réunion Island) and Madagascar, looks dissonant in its pairing with the Comoros, these other islands of the Indian Ocean, even though it also grows there. I peer closer at the sachet. Presiding over the name, in smaller letters, I read: DAVENPORT AND SONS MASTER TEA BLENDERS. Even more intriguing and incongruous: the tropical, archipelagic tea is under the aegis of a staunchly New England name.

I am waiting for Nigel. I supplement my partial doctoral scholarship by tutoring high school and college kids. Nigel is neither. He is a musician who wants to speak French fluently, before his band tours the Caribbean with Martinican and Guadeloupean artists. While I ponder the disparate islands that conspire to bring us together – from Nigel's touring locations to the implied provenances of my tea – he arrives. He waves, all smiles and ease. I find out that he is American despite his British name, and that he loves tea despite his country's predilection for coffee. All these cultural nuances I have acquired in the five years I have lived here, at the same time shedding so many of my own. I have traded oiled-up tresses and dark skin turned ashy from skin-lightening creams for the sea-, sand- and sun-kissed images that dance in the eyes of most Americans when I tell them I am from an island.

I allow myself to flirt a little during those first months I tutor Nigel. He has a very easy, very white smile. The night he returns to Manhattan from Martinique he calls me, and I invite him to my apartment while my housemates are out. He smiles in the dim light of the bedroom, and I remember that his teeth are very straight, very white, somehow accentuated by his frayed sweater and faded jeans. He wears old clothes the way rich people do, a carefully curated aesthetics of poverty. I kiss his open smile then, taking it all in, the ways he has fucked and loved gorgeous men and women, the ways he owns spaces that push against mine, the not-quite-white of his Sicilian ancestors, laundered after Ellis Island, the unburden of his every day.

As he kisses me back, his greedy mouth searching for an opening, his hand slides down my stomach looking for the same, finding it quickly. I will his fingers in, revelling in the easy authority with which he moves in the world and in me. I turn my face and my aching throat to the wall, even as my sex pulls me toward his virtuoso fingers, all dexterity and controlled passion.

He stops then. His fingers, still inside, suddenly still. He puts his mouth to my ear and demands: I want to hear it. He has found my tongue, but does not find my voice. I stretch tall, silent, as I come in staccato, anticipating what his fingers are a proxy for. And desiring what his white teeth and blue eyes and accent are metonyms for.

When we have sex, my moans and postures are as deliberately arranged as my words. They come from years of watching Jason Priestley, Andie MacDowell, Shah Rukh Khan and Rani Mukherjee speak love in English, dubbed in French. The words I actually want to say never make it to my tongue, which has by now fossilised into pointed and squared morphologies. They escape me once in a while, but always outside of sexual intercourse.

Ayo, that protean sauce of an onomatopoeia that goes with every dish, comes first to express sheer pleasure, utter disappointment, and everything in between. Then fouf, more and more impatience. After a fight one day, something long forgotten almost escapes my lips: bour to sime ale. The painful knot in my throat alchemises the words and translates to Nigel: it's over. He moves out of my apartment the same day. Although we break up on my terms, we say it in his words. That's why it's over.

I still go to the campus tearoom. When Vandana sees me on my own, she comes over to chat and asks where Nigel is. I think of the long, intimate relationship language and sex have had in my bed, of the French we loved to flirt in and the Creole – Mauritian, Martinican or Guadeloupean – he never bothered to learn. But instead, I raise my voice and say, intending to shock: I don't know how to say "fuck me hard" in Creole.

I expect Vandana to recoil or, at least, look away. Deadpan, she tells me how, and even adds her own spin on it. I recoil and look away. I have only ever heard these words used in violence toward women. They sting like a slap, and their shape remains imprinted on my cheek for a while.

That night, the pleasure in my groin moves upward and explodes on my tongue, suddenly unsilenced, in words finally unviolenced.

Bour mwa for, ziska mo sousout bate.

I come as I breathe in the tea scent lodged in Vandana's hair: Vanilla Comoros.

Vandana whose mother raised her on her own, working night shifts at a tea factory, cursing in Creole just like the men.

Vandana who is also her mother's daughter.

●　　●　　●

Feast your eyes on the authentic vista of green tea bushes and local women picking tea while enjoying a tasting from the comfort of our colonial teahouse. Begin with our airy and refreshing

vanilla tea, a favourite among customers, and
end with the bold and complex Gold Label.

∗ ∗ ∗

When I visit Dadi with Mama and Papa, I pretend not to like her, because Mama does not like her. Mama blames her mother-in-law for her husband's temper. But Dadi knows how to win me over. She beckons to me with the hundred-rupee note she keeps hidden in the folds of her sari. She wraps my fist quickly around the note and urges me to hide it in my pocket, all the while whispering conspiratorially as if she is entrusting me with a treasure. She feeds me dal puri and tea with heaps of sugar. She swallows her own dal puri with a generous dose of arrack, but not before having poured a libation on the floor for Somoreeah. I laugh as she calls me Durga, rolling and trilling the *r* in her Mauritian Bhojpuri. I do not know Bhojpuri and she barely speaks Creole, but the way she says my name is another gift with which she tells me she loves me.

I like it most when Papa takes me, without Mama, to the plantation at the end of Dadi's shift. Dadi puts me in the basket hanging on her back, on top of fresh tea leaves, so that I can see the large colonial house on the hill, beyond the rows of tea bushes on the Bois Chéri estate. There are people coming in and out of the house. Although they are the ones who look like ants, it is Papa who seems to become small next to me. I want to become small too, but on Dadi's shoulders I am an extension of her strong, tall frame, and I cannot. The scent in her hair comforts me, as she silently picks tea to fulfil her quota.

Dadi started picking tea when she was nine. She picked tea twice as fast as her husband, earned more than him. And at home, she was twice as likely to lose her temper, especially after a few glasses of arrack. She would tell him bour to sime ale, get the fuck out of my house.

She stopped working on the tea plantation when she was seventy. But she did not lose the tea-picking basket, still weighing down her back despite its absence. When I visit from the US she walks toward me, bent almost at a right angle at the waist, the six-foot powerhouse that she once was now barely three feet tall, the height of a child. She unknots a corner of her sari and produces a hundred-rupee note for me, even as I protest that I am now a professor. She smiles, not understanding my words, my work, my world. But it does not matter when she hides the note in my hand and says my name.

The last time I visit Dadi before her death, she unknots a corner of her sari, but instead of the usual hundred-rupee note, she shoves into my hand a couple of pages, whispering in her usual way, gesturing for me to put them away.

A few days later, I stand in front of the pyre where Dadi lies as if sleeping. The eldest son or grandson traditionally lights the pyre, but Papa did not leave her any grandson, so I hold the torch. Later that day, I dig into my bag and find the papers she gave me. My aunt recognises them. She tells me they are the only official document left of my paternal ancestors. They arrived in Mauritius from Bihar, replacing the enslaved on sugarcane plantations after the abolition of slavery. Dadi must have asked a distant relative who works in the National Archives to do her a favour. This is the only written testament of the couple from whom we are all descended. But the enormity of the situation does not correspond to the sparse two pages I hold in my hands. All columns and lists, they look like they were taken from our old grocer's ledger. As I peer closer, instead of oil, rice and flour bought on credit, I see the names of coolies borrowed on colonial contract. Next to each name, butchered by French orthography, cold details: registration number, provenance, age, height.

A painful knot forms in my throat when my eyes see before I can understand: HEIGHT: 3 FEET 2 INCHES. When he arrives on the island in 1880, he is six years old. He has a first name only, the same that will become our surname, the same that my secondary-school teacher will replace with funny ones during roll call. I look at the other page. She arrives a few years later, the same year tea is introduced in Mauritius. Her name is Somoreeah. She is five, and spends three weeks in a depot before being sent to the Bois Chéri plantation. The sparse documents bring more questions than answers. But they do tell me that she is three feet five inches. She is tall, taller even than him.

● ● ●

Some altars housed statues and images of goddesses, garlanded with flowers. Others held pungent incense and the photographs and personal belongings of dear departed ones. For Durga, we, her teas, held her dear ones, her goddesses.

When her daughter turned five, Durga took her to Mauritius, and to the plantation where Dadi had worked as a métayère, a sharecropper, in the last years of her life. Mama accompanied them but stayed in the car on the side of the road. Her daughter hanging on her shoulders, Durga waded into the waist-high leaves as Mama advised caution on land that they did not own, land she said had only been rented to Dadi. Voices from the colonial house drifted down toward them, muted, but they were quickly drowned out as the leaves tickled the feet of the five-year old and she laughed. Pointing to the tea leaves, she asked: ki ete sa? What is this?

Standing tall over the bushes, Durga breathed in the humid, pungent scent and replied, dite.

WHAT BURNS

JULIE BOUCHARD

Translated from the French by Arielle Aaronson

1

First burns the boreal forest, up in the north. A little south of that burns the woman. Around her burn a tortoise, a pair of Siamese cats, two caged birds, a dozen mice and seven other people whom misfortune trapped inside the nineteenth-century heritage building. What a tragedy. Eventually, the building collapses on itself. *Oof.* Oh, and don't forget what's burned for decades, what's still burning, what will burn: all the oil, the coal, the gas. What else? Other than Dora, who will burn sometime around noon to much less fanfare. With help from Franz, presently asleep on his couch, who will lovingly slide Dora into the oven when the time comes. For now, Dora is left to cool in a refrigerated space. Perfect. Now let's continue counting the fires. Since, thousands of kilometres east of the boreal forest and the woman, the pets, the mice, Franz, and Dora, in the face of our obscene helplessness, the flames will soon destroy musical instruments – a violin, a guitar, a tabla – stuffed into barrels scattered here and there throughout the public square. Madness. Finally, at the bitter end of the hottest day on record, any remaining illusions we've clung to are reduced to ash in a burst of spontaneous combustion – this one, that one, one more. In a word: welcome, on this memorable summer solstice 2023, to what burns. Come closer. Make yourself uncomfortable, right there, in front of me. Perfect. And together, foreheads sweating, let's watch the world incandesce.

2

But before we send the fire engines racing down Main Street, before we dispatch the airtankers and chinooks to drop thousands of litres of

water onto the forest canopy, and right before
Franz, who has finally woken up, heats the
oven to 1,040 degrees Celsius, let's talk about
what doesn't burn on June 21. The downstairs
neighbour's toast, rescued from the toaster at
the last moment, doesn't burn. Excellent. The
pressure-treated wood of her sister-in-law's deck
will never go up in flames, either. Incredible. And
the sofa where Franz was sleeping – our Franz,
who slowly unfolds himself and shuffles over to
the sink, bending low to splash water on his face
– was coated with a flame retardant that protects
it from fire but contaminates the air. Great. As
for the concrete that dominates the entryway of
every house on Main Street, it's made of a non-
combustible material. Wonderful. Oh, I forgot:
one last living thing doesn't burn today. A special
thing. A sacred thing. What is it? You, of course.
Sitting there. You don't burn. No.

3

Because your discomfort at the end of the
first paragraph saved you from the fire. It did.

Since you live – or, rather, used to live – in that nineteenth-century heritage building. You can thank the story for distracting you, if only for a moment, and sheltering you, here, from what burns. I suspect you were paid to be there, so near to it. Or you were promised a starring role in "What Burns". Whatever it was that spared you from the worst, the bottom line is that *this* is your only refuge for now because you, poor you, no longer have a home. Terrible, isn't it? Nothing left to remind you of who you once were. No childhood photo albums, clothes, or even shoes. You lost, in the process, your karate diploma (fourth-*dan* black belt), your dead sister's gold ring (Virginia, what a looker), your entire library (including your Thomas Bernhard, your Flannery O'Connor, your Kafka) and the lock of blond hair your mother snipped when you were six, which you treasured in a clear plastic bag. So, tell me: who are you, now, without all of these objects that shaped your world? What will become of you, now that the fire has ravaged you? *Oops.* Now big crocodile tears are streaming down your face. I'll try this to console you: at least you're alive. That's something. *We* are alive. You, me, Franz and the rest of them. Unlike the woman. The woman on the Persian rug, on the second floor of the nineteenth-century heritage building.

4

The woman is wearing chic black slacks cut from a high-quality fabric, a black jacket of the same cloth, and an ivory blouse. A pair of size-41 stilettos dangle from her feet. Wrapped around her fingers, a fourteen-karat gold chain winks in the light. The woman's inanimate body lies on the Persian rug in the living room, which is located on the second floor of the nineteenth-century heritage building, which isn't – what a shame – up to code in the city of M. In fact, some apartments lack both an emergency exit and a sprinkler system. Illegal. All this incredible illegality, and all the complications that arise from it will be settled – or not – in a few months, by several lawyers. The owner of the heritage building will sue the city of M. for its overly strict renovation rules. Relatives of the eight victims will sue the owner for renting out apartments that didn't meet the city's building standards. The city of M. will deny all responsibility. Airbnb will continue to encourage owners to rent out their apartments to tourists, contributing to a city-wide housing crisis.

5

Let's return to the woman lying on the Persian rug in the living room, and to the man standing over her – because there is also a man in the room. The man grabs a bottle of fire accelerant and pours its contents over the woman, the furniture, the Persian rug, the plants, the walls, the books. Then he takes a matchbook from his pocket, tears away a flimsy poplar stick and strikes the head, coated in antimony trisulfide, manganese dioxide and potassium chlorate, against the strip of powdered glass and red phosphorus on the back of the book on which, if you come a little closer, you can read HÔTEL NELLIGAN – AN UNFORGETTABLE EXPERIENCE in red lettering. Then the man casually drops the match and exits the heritage building through the main entrance. He stops a little further on, takes out a cigarette and smokes it under the harsh light of a streetlamp as he watches the building go up in flames. In the scorching early-morning air, the sound of sirens approaches. Once they arrive, 150 firefighters unroll hoses, raise ladders and train their nozzles onto the inferno with breathless efficiency and, like heroes, wielding axes and wearing face masks, enter the burning nineteenth-century heritage building that will require nine hours to secure.

6

Warning: we'll never find the arsonist. The man who walks nonchalantly through the streets of M. We'll never know what vengeance sustains him, or how such fury can come to inhabit a man's body and mind. Nor will we ever work out his relationship to the woman, what the gold chain represents or the significance of the matchbook from the Hôtel Nelligan, located 100 metres from the nineteenth-century heritage building. You shake your head, dismayed by this flagrant lack of information. Say: *I don't believe it.* Add angrily: *How can you?* End with a judgment: *It's unconscionable.* Alas, I have absolutely no authority over meaning. You'll have to make do with what's been given while I attempt to describe, for the purposes of the unfolding narrative, what remains of the heritage building while Franz is just sitting down to breakfast.

7

By the time the weary firefighters return to their stations, all that's left behind is a sad and charred stone skeleton punctuated by holes through which the dense, grey sky is visible. Within, cool the ashes of a tortoise, two cats, two birds, a few mice and eight bodies, including that of the woman on the Persian rug who burned alive and who, yes, resembled you. You start coughing, sniffling. Your skull feels like it's in a vice. Your eyes sting. You attribute these symptoms to the powerful smell of smoke, a smell now mingling with a complex blend of gas, particulates and water vapour produced by the forest fires 1,000 kilometres north of the heritage building that strong winds have blown all the way here. This noxious substance – which will reach New York by tomorrow and prevent Joe Jr from taking his morning jog through Central Park – seeps into your lungs, your veins, your soul. And as the entire city of M. wakes to the smell of catastrophe, you beg me to take us away, please, from "What Burns". Unfortunately, that isn't possible. Since "What Burns" burns everywhere. Even there. Look. Look up.

8

See that? The boreal forest. Proud dominion, to the north of Canada's 50th parallel. Ever come this far up? I can't imagine you have. Then we should take the opportunity to admire, from the tip of our new, collective eco-anxiety, the topmost branches of the balsam fir where lightning will strike. Isn't it a beautiful tree? The most northerly fir tree that exists. The last time you saw one like it, you say with a lump in your throat, colourful ornaments hung from its branches and a garland of lights strangled it (this is the first image that comes to mind), blinking on and off at regular intervals. You recall that at the foot of the tree sat a single wrapped gift, the symbol of infinite solitude, though you don't say whether it was one you'd received or were planning to give. To your left, through the window of the heritage building, you could see rain falling at an angle. To your right, beyond the party wall, in the spot where a woman would soon burn alive on a Persian rug, you could hear Ella Fitzgerald singing "Have Yourself a Merry Little Christmas". An empty champagne glass in one hand, mind and heart swelling with mixed emotions, you sat cross-legged in front of the tree and opened the aforementioned gift. A fourteen-karat gold chain. Then, standing in front of your gold-plated bathroom mirror, you fastened the chain around your neck and stared at your reflection, as you would a stranger, for a long moment. You've since developed a habit of twisting the chain around your right index finger as you talk, listen, dream, fret ... like you're doing now. Oh, but – no. You're not wearing it. You must have forgotten it, just before joining me at the edge of what burns, on the bedside table, next to your queen-sized bed, on the second floor of what used to be the heritage building. The beautiful fourteen-karat gold chain you loved so much. And this reminds you that you've lost everything. Even yourself.

9

Lost among 307 million hectares of woodlands that represent about 9 percent of the world's forests, seven thousand forest fires are currently burning – fires which, under normal circumstances, would never even cross your mind. You try to picture the scope of 307 million hectares, but you can't. And you suddenly feel tiny, irrelevant. The thunder blast ravages your tender ears and, through a strange and subtle effect of bodily reverberation, rattles your remaining faith in love, death, Christmas, the world, yourself. Pity. But let's get back to the matter at hand: the sky. Building within a cumulonimbus cloud formed in air as unstable as the times, the electrical discharge, following the shortest path to the ground, strikes the tip of the balsam – *whoooooosh* – travels down to its roots – *zoooooom* – heating the sap along the way – *hisssssss* – and sets the trunk ablaze – *shhhhhhhh*. What a show. Asleep in one of the topmost branches of the tree, where a few days ago a Tennessee warbler meticulously and painstakingly built its nest, five baby birds are killed instantly. Their mother, who was returning to her brood, beak filled with food, reverses course and chirps off through the chromatic field, passing in turn splashes of oranges, strawberry reds ringed with methylene blue, splendid jade greens against a cobalt background. In all directions, magnificent larches, century-old pines, white birches, black spruces, maples and yews ignite. Around the imposing crown of fire created by the flaming treetops, you can hear the beating wings and panicked cries of hundreds of vireos, thrushes, wrens, grosbeaks, sparrows and flycatchers as they take to the air – along with the mother warbler, whose recent loss prompts you to contemplate, through anthropomorphic bias, her despair. On the ground now, hundreds of animals are trying to flee; a family of woodland caribou is overtaken by the flames. Few will make it out alive, save a handful of insects, lizards and a dozen deer mice who were quick – *bravo!* – to find refuge underground. Careful – we should move away from the fires, try to save what's left of our skin.

10

According to experts' calculations, the fire is advancing at around 500 metres a day. In less than forty-eight hours, and unless weather conditions change, the town of K., located on the edge of the forest, will be engulfed in flames, too. Mayor Bauer, scarcely two months in office and already facing one of the biggest challenges of her career, sits with tousled hair behind the microphone at the local radio station to issue an evacuation order. She is confident, composed. *Take only what you need. Some clothes. Your pets. Money.* She reassures the residents. Police officers, stationed strategically along the road with spare gas tanks to make sure no car will run out, are watering the asphalt periodically to prevent it from overheating. What would normally be a three-hour trip might now, with the sudden traffic, take twenty hours. *Don't forget to pack snacks. Be patient, dear citizens. Don't panic. Everything will be fine.* Will it, really? Franz reaches for this additional optimism and turns off the radio. He won't panic. He's never panicked in his life, not even when everything was falling apart. Not even when they learned Dora had only a few months to live. Besides, he's just spilled strawberry jam on his white shirt. And he's not panicking.

11

You interrupt me as Franz is changing his shirt – go ahead, don't be shy – to undermine "What Burns" by mentioning your climate-sceptic cousin, Johnny D. Who doesn't believe, hang on, who doesn't believe in forest fires.

Oh. Good. Lord. You pull out a notebook and pencil, think for a minute, take notes. Look up. Think some more. Write some more. Since the first paragraph, you've experienced a gradual transformation. Now here you are, inspired, invested. You're wholly committed to this trial by fire. You want to 'change the world'. Really? OK. You believe in yourself. Congratulations. *The world is on fire!* you cry. Um, yes. That's exactly what – but you cut me off. The clock is ticking. At your next family reunion, you'll try to convince your climate-sceptic cousin of the urgency to act, you'll pull out the statistics. Look at this number, at that number. You'll point to this graph, to that fact. *See how many hectares burned this year alone? Doesn't that prove ...? Shouldn't we ...? Perhaps we can try ...?* Your phone is ringing. It's him. Johnny D. What a coincidence. He's heard about the fire in the nineteenth-century heritage building and knows you live there. You hesitate to answer. You want to tell Johnny about everything – the numbers, the facts, the fires, our dismay, of course. But not over the phone. So, you don't answer. Or, rather, your silence does the answering for you.

12

Their voices had been ignored for years. Their suggestions dismissed. Their appeals rejected. The result? After a vote to strike, they decided, on December 25 – just as you slipped between the cold cotton sheets of your queen-sized bed for a night that would prove sleepless, wearing nothing but the fourteen-karat gold chain around your neck – to close the immense wrought-iron gates of the cemetery in the town of K. In the meantime, they placed the bodies – forty-three, including Dora's – in cold storage, tucked off to the right, behind the three cremation ovens. For months, strikers had kept the cemetery closed to bereaved families, holding up picket signs with slogans: CEMETERY EMPLOYEES ARE BURIED UNDER INEQUITY! MORTALLY DETERMINED TO GET JUSTICE! EVEN THE GHOSTS SUPPORT US! They wanted better working conditions, and shouted their demands from dawn till dusk as they paced back and forth in front of the gates. Decent salaries. Stable hours. At the very minimum, latex gloves for handling the bodies. And to be informed ahead of time, please, if a body was to arrive in a state of decomposition – those found in vacant lots, for instance – so they'd have time to protect themselves against the nauseating smell of putrefaction that might otherwise line their throats for days. But their requests fell on deaf ears.

13

Meanwhile, the cemetery groundhogs had burrowed into the soil, dug tunnels and found bones that they'd unearthed, shifted, gnawed. Grass had grown wild all over the grounds, covering stone statues, wooden crosses, plaster angels, a few ghosts. Begonias and carnations had withered beside the gravestones. Some distraught mourners had taken to jumping the fence at night. Others squeezed underneath. All they wanted, after all, was to pay their respects to the dead. And nobody was going to stop them.

Interviewed on the six o'clock news, a teary-eyed Georges Zapatakis declared, "I promised my mother she'd be laid to rest beside her husband, but now they've got her in a warehouse on ice. It keeps me up at night." Just yesterday, a tentative agreement was approved, with 83 percent of the vote. *Hooray!* Georges Zapatakis applauded. All cemetery workers were expected back on the job today, June 21. That is, until the fire foils their plan and Mayor Bauer orders everyone to evacuate. The line of cars stretches along Route 183. Behind the wheel of his Chevrolet, Georges Zapatakis starts crying again. Within half a day, all residents of K. will be evacuated. Except for Franz, who had promised Dora as he held her hand on December 25 that he would look after her bones.

14

Dora. She's intrigued you since the beginning. And while you were talking about Johnny D. and I was telling you about the strike, and while the entire town of K. was sitting bumper-to-bumper along Route 183, Franz was walking towards her and taking note of all the humble life around him. The mature ash tree to his left, Mr Gary's rosebush a bit further up the road, the orange sky above, the empty storefront of Madame Wang's boutique, the hydrangeas framing the front door of Mayor Bauer's house, a stray cat and the Poirier and Picard families loading bags into the trunks of their cars. When he finally reaches the end of humble life, Franz opens the thick metal door of the crematorium. On the other side, he slips on long, green latex gloves, removes the cardboard box from the cold room, places it on a stainless steel lift table, opens it to see Dora, whispers a few words into her ear, gives her a kiss and slips a metal tag into the box before closing it. Number 153. In twenty-one years, Franz has cremated nearly 6,000 bodies, honouring the wishes of the dead. Dora's will be the last one he burns, honouring this last promise.

15

Curious about Franz and Dora, you ask me to expand. *Go ahead,* you say. *Spill. I want details.*

You come dangerously close to the abyss of "What Burns". Now, I have to warn you, you're starting to wear my patience thin. Shouldn't you know, at your age, that there's no point in seeking an autopsy of love – any love? Yet you persist, you can't just leave it at that. I'm not sure I follow you. At what? *At that,* you repeat. Without adding anything about Dora (the colour of her hair, what kind of person she was, what killed her), about Franz (how he loved her, what words he used, whether or not he bought her flowers) and about how they were together. It's one thing to scatter clues, you say furiously, that lead nowhere in "What Burns". To tell us we might never find the arsonist. To hear that Mayor Bauer issued an evacuation order, that's only natural. But to ask us to invent love is – and this is your second judgment – a major plot hole. You cross your arms. Turn your back on me. You – well, I never! You're sulking.

16

Since you're still facing the crematorium door, you won't see the living Franz slide the late Dora into the oven. Pity. Neither will you watch as Franz transforms over the two hours that Dora burns. You won't see his handsome brown head dip forward, his shoulders droop, his delicate right hand find his heavy heart, his blue eyes glaze over, his broad frame shudder. Worse still: you won't witness the only poetic image that could have reconciled you with "What Burns", as Franz opens the oven door to reveal, like a strange work of art, Dora's bones glowing red.

17

To help fight the wildfires, reinforcements arrive from around the world (150 from South Korea, 200 for the United States, 30 from Portugal, 100 from France) and set to work as soon as they land, marking out lines of defence as a containment strategy. In the city of M., municipal police cordon off the nineteenth-century heritage building with yellow CAUTION tape, and experts are dispatched to the scene to gather information, possibly even evidence of foul play. Detectives also question local residents; some claim they saw a strange man hanging around the building right after the fire broke out. As for the residents of K., nearly all have been evacuated – except for Franz, of course, who is busy grinding Dora's bones and who, we anticipate, will not have time to outrun the flames. You finally turn to face me. You almost forgot why you were angry. After all, you say, you are, and I am, just a storyteller. It's true. You walk over to Franz and discover, right there among Dora's ashes, a red-hot metal tag with the number 153 that you pick up and intend to keep, you tell me, your voice full of emotion, as a souvenir of "What Burned".

18

They say that after the fire, insects, drawn to the smell of smoke, will be the first to return to the forest, to lay their eggs. Then birds will follow, arriving in flocks. A few weeks later, trailblazing plant life, the first to colonise the scorched earth, will also begin to take root. Animals living nearby will eventually return to their natural habitat. Despite everything, life will rise from the ashes.

By the way, I heard you found a new apartment
in the city of M. I'm glad. You go on to tell me
that your fourteen-karat gold chain was found
intact amid the charred debris. A miracle. You
also admit that you now keep the number 153
on you at all times, tucked in your back pocket.
Great idea. You eventually ask me if, among the
ashes of the town of K., we ever found those of
Franz. Unfortunately, I don't know the answer.
But you no longer hold that against me. Thank
you. So you decide to picture Franz mingled in
with the rest, not far from Dora. Why not? Now,
all that's left is for me to strike a match, hold the
flame to the heart of "What Burns" and watch as
meaning turns into white smoke.

THE DEVIL'S SON

PORTIA SUBRAN

After hearing a phrase of music, memory suddenly rises in front of you like the clearing mist of the blue Northern Range.

The heavy smoke of pitch-oil flambeaux.

The smell of rain on warm asphalt in the night.

The wail of your father. The silence of your mother.

Some nights you will not forget, even though you feel you bury it deep enough.

Is a brand to the back of your skull, somehow still burning, still on fire, hiding up in layers of flesh, follicles, a web of nerves. Then suddenly it come back to malign your mind with misery and guilt.

Is like that for me now, stick up in traffic on the way to San Fernando, and a station start to play a song that feel like a knife plunge in my belly.

Me eh know what old-time disc jockey dig up this old-time song from my youth. Gogi Grant's "The Wayward Wind".

The song is a pull to my navel string. The way eating the flesh of the armoured cascadura does call you to come back home to die in Trinidad, that song pull my soul back to Chaguanas.

Old Chaguanas, from sixty years back. A flood of memories erupting and fighting for the spotlight in my mind – the smell of burning sugarcane and rotting bagasse, that scent like festering flesh. The splash of cold water from a gleaming copper basin on the days that boiled us in sweat, roaming through the rows of Woodford Lodge estate looking for adventure. The sizzling crack of a film projector, the unnatural firmness and coldness of the Anglican cemetery.

The bellowing of a bison, his voice vibrating down the thick muscles of his neck. The Chaguanas I did only know about was the one from the early Fifties, when a talk did start up 'bout electricity coming to the village. Back then it was a village, but *oui papa*, today them does call it a *borough*.

To help we understand what this electricity did mean, they had was to set up a Delco generator and a silver screen in the Woodford Lodge Cricket Field to play a flim.

I could remember that day good, man. Me and my pardna Jaikaran had gone down early in the morning to gawk at the equipment. A huge scaffold coming down where the cricket fielders woulda be posted. A string of bulbs wrapped around the massive appamat trees, an untethered silk screen whipping out in the breeze. And reel, man, reel ah flim offloading from a cart.

We ask the man, what it have dey on them flim?

He say it go show a man and his wife tending to a farm with the use of something none of we had – electricity. The flim wasn't meant to be science fiction, but it did feel like that way to we.

We did live in darkness. If you did forget to light your home flambeau, you was getting suck into the oblivion every night.

Papa did tell me it was a good thing that we was going to get electricity, because the kinda darkness we in, it does let the mind run mad with superstition.

Papa was a logical man who did follow the *see it and believe it* platitude of life. Mammy was the opposite – according to my Pa, she find great solace in the greatest superstition of all – religion. Never see a woman so deeply committed to the tenets of the Church and feel she self more missionary than parishioner. She favourite story revolve round the evangelising and conversion of the savages.

But here in the heart of Chaguanas, it didn't have no such savages, so she find them in she own children. She had us reading the Bible every morning, covering it end-to-end every three years. Up to now, I can quote everything from the wrath of Elijah to the temptations of Christ.

And as much as she believe in the angels, Mammy believe even more in the Devil. She listen to every tale of myth, spirit and monster, and did know of every practised way to outwit a demon.

86

Rub dog yampi in your eye, look through a keyhole and you would see a lagahoo.

If you meet La Diablesse, strip yourself naked, turn your clothes inside out and put them on again, she eh go seem to trace you after that. To see a soucouyant, put fowl shit in your eye and watch up in the night sky.

That last one, I make it up, but I sure I could ketch my mother with it.

Mammy did feed on every tale the neighbours had about the strange things they see while walking home in the night. The latest one was from Brother Lal, a fellow parishioner from two streets over. A few nights earlier, he did come across a bison while walking home from the train station. The bison was standing up on two hind legs at the crossroads beneath a wide spreading samaan tree. He mouth was open long and low, almost big enough like a man could crawl in. The beast give a long, wide grin – teeth glittering in a rod of moonlight, glittering like gold. When he watch good, this bison whole mouth was full of gold teeth. The lips curl back and a deep baritone voice rumble from the belly of the beast and ask, *"How you coming home so late, Lal?"*

Brother Lal say he dunno if he grow wing and fly, but he reach home in a panic and fall down in front he gate.

Mammy hold a long prayer session the next night for Brother Lal and he family, with she own offspring as congregation in tow. Brother Lal look like he couldn't even raise up he head good, cold sweating on a bench under a pitch-oil lamp. He big daughter sitting on a peerha, massaging he foot.

"The Devil doesn't come in person, he too full of spite and shame and laziness," Mammy say. "He does always send he son, that is who Lal see that night."

"Minds running mad with superstition," Papa say. He eh even try to whisper self.

Mammy never take he on, nah. She see so much children dying of Obeah-inflicted polio, and *maljeaux* tuberculosis, that she give she first-born child a name that would strike fear into the hearts of any demon. To ensure the protection of any scion to follow.

The name was *Gabriel*, and that unfortunate first-born was me.

As the oldest sibling, I always had to walk with a horde of children – three boys and five girls. Me at the head, bearing the name that meant *Warrior of God*.

We use to walk in order of birth. To church, to school. Eventually the line start to look uneven when my brother Isaac, then thirteen, just three years younger than me, had a potent growth spurt. A whole head taller than me.

He throw everything off balance. He whole existence used to throw me off balance. If I say *A*, Isaac went with *B*.

He was prone to what he did call *adventures*, like if he had an irrepressible pull to wander every trace and tributary contained in Chaguanas. He go come up to me and say, "Boy, you hear it have wildcat in De Verteuil Estate?"

"Boy, it eh ha no wildcat there," I go say.

But come Saturday evening, this boy cover up in mud and scratch, eyes wide, mouth spreading, belly big with laugh, telling me he see the wildcat.

What I go say, Isaac live up to the meaning of his name, *He Will Laugh*. You couldn't tell him to do nothing, no chore at all, he done disappear for the next adventure, and more laugh.

He exist without any kind of responsibility, waltzing and chirruping, full of songs, his favourite one being fit for his ceaseless wandering – Gogi Grant's "The Wayward Wind". And then every lick of trouble he get into, it was the Warrior of God collecting the blame and an even share of the licks.

Brother Lal was usually the one marching down to we house on Taitt Street to give my mother the scoop on what she eight children was doing that day. We did always know he was coming down the street when he start calling out, *"Sister Ragbir! Sister Ragbir!"*

That day I was in the yard, repairing a spade for my job with Mr Beharry by the cemetery. It was a few years now I was working there with Jaikaran and some other boys around All Souls, fixing up the graves for the family and them to light they candle. Something about the slow decomposition of Chaguanas's dead Anglicans did make the soil like steel, and plenty times I did find myself having to replace the handle of my spade.

Around noon, Brother Lal find he way into the yard. He settled heself on the wooden stool near the half-open dutch doors.

"Sister Ragbir, I had was to tell you!" And so he start.

While taking he morning constitution round the neighbourhood, he stop at the Invictus Cricket Field to watch an ongoing match. And lo, he see Isaac squatting under the stands, creeping from spot to spot, like if is penny he was gathering up. Is only when Brother Lal stop to wipe he brow, he ketch that Isaac was quietly snatching up the cigarette butts as soon as the livid patrons was dropping them – collecting and then taking a long pull from each.

Mammy face look like somebody smash she head with a Coke bottle. She thank him, wait for him to leave, then tell me to bring Isaac from the back of the house.

He was there staring into a huge puddle from the rain all the nights before. The water was tea-coloured, stained from all the leaves that did continuously fall into it. Isaac's hair was slick back with a dollop of petroleum jelly, he hand caressing the water, fingers sieving for inky tadpoles.

He touch he chin for a moment, a bristle of adolescent hair now emerging. When I call for him he look up doe-eye at me, but I pull him up rough, and haul him over by he magga shoulders to stand in front of Mammy. I lean against the wall, my ropey arm cross over my chest, waiting for she to let Isaac have it.

Instead she say, "Where you was, Gabriel?"

Me? Where *I* was?

I shoulda know I was coming as God's Warrior again, to protect this wotless child. I coulda lie, is only natural to protect yourself from danger – but I couldn't manage to lie to my mother.

I confess to liming with Jaikaran. Silence hanging in the air now. Mammy looking up at me, and Isaac gazing down. I start to explain, "Checking out the screen set up for the flim tonight –"

She hand slide down she shin, unhouse a leather slipper from she foot and *wallop! wallop!* I collect two hard slap in my face.

"Watching them set up a *Devil's Screen!*" she start she bawling. "This is why you wasn't watching the chile!"

I bow down my head, face burning like if a thousand jep now land their stingers on it. She push a hard hand on each one of we shoulder and had we on we knees.

Mammy did not give lecture. She did give sermon. Describing to us the ways in which the Devil's influence could leave the screen and pour into the mind of us, the innocent.

The Devil's House, that was what she did call Jubilee Cinema – a half-mile up the road from our house. Sometimes me and Jaikaran would break biche from work and bolt up the road to see the latest flim. Jubilee was a small, smoke-filled theatre, powered by a generator. The cheapest seat we coulda afford was pit, sitting right in front the screen, you break your neck backwards to see Rita Hayworth tempting Tyrone Power in *Blood and Sand.* If that was the Devil's House, then of course the setup in the grounds was call the *Devil's Screen*.

Mammy bang she fist on the butcher's board in place of a pulpit and we was sentenced to memorise Matthew Chapter 4, Verses 1–11: *Then Jesus was led by the Spirit into the wilderness to be tempted by the Devil.* We was to repeat it until she finish cook lunch.

I watch Isaac staring at the ceiling. A small smile creeping on he face.

I watch this boy, his voice turning to a sing-song thing.

I watch, and even though I couldna do it then, I imagine slapping him repeatedly, keeping rhythm with the verse. Again and again and again. And I just thinking, *this boy does get to live he life, and I does have to get punish for it.*

* * *

Working in the cemetery for Mr Beharry was gruelling. Twelve o'clock hot sun, sweat like the river of Jordan down your back, you could get delusional like you hearing voices from the graves. Especially on All Souls. Me and Jaikaran never understand how the rain coulda be pouring, and the earth of the grave couldn't get any softer. New pools of water did erupt under we every day, so we was always dodging them while trying to finish the people wok.

We did also have to watch out for Mr Beharry's ill-behaved grey bison – whom he affectionately call Beta. And my God, the man did love the bull like he own son.

But the bison didn't like nobody, not even Mr Beharry.

In my mind, taking a page from my mother book, Beta real name was "the Devil's Son".

Beta didn't want nobody crossing into what he perceive to be *he* land, walking through them fields near the cemetery. His permanent seat of residence was under the swinging branches of the jamun tree grove, slurping up the fallen berries, his muzzle permanently stained bright violet. Spat out the seeds right on the edge of the deep, deep ravine.

To be honest, nobody want to go near that ravine anyhow. We was lucky we was in the rainy season, it was always full of water, but then Mr Beharry did tell we, the bodies of them long-dead Anglicans does push out, and if you look hard in the dry season, that ravine floor full of bleach-white bones.

Sometimes we would take a little ease up, sitting on the generously broad headstone of Mr Lowen Bullen, ketch kicks on he name. Wondering who Mr Lowen was bulling there in the afterlife.

Where we wanted to be, though, was under them jamun trees to ketch a break, but that was Beta liming spot, stretch out and shaded under long, thin boughs of the jamun trees – a massive pile of grey folded flesh, eyes like fire. Snorting out gusts of dust and phlegm, like something out of Stan Jones's mind, a bison from the Devil's Herd.

Jaikaran say Beta never properly get break in with the yoke. Instead, he nearly kill the man who try to train him.

Young bison does be out and bad, fierce and strong. Them could release a man from he life easy, easy, unless you break them in. Yoking them to a silk cotton buttress, let him run like the enraged beast he is for an hour or two, until he settle down to the docility of a lamb.

But Beta never settle.

He ploughed through the estate, head drive down low into the ground, scooping men up, throwing them off the crown of his horns. I hear he did pierce one man, and the foot had to cut off from the gangrene. But Jaikaran did tell me, *The horn eh so bad, is the tongue that worse. That a bison tongue could lick the flesh off a man, as easy as peeling silk fig.*

Devil ting, I telling you.

Jaikaran say they was going and slaughter him for beef, but Mr Beharry couldn't let that happen and say he would mind him, keep him as a watchman for the graveyard. And is true.

I never see Beta pull no cart, drag no plough, anyway. The bison's job was to stare at we. Make sure we wasn't slacking.

●　●　●

That night, Mammy was protesting – I coulda hear she from the roadside, going on about how they did set up a Devil's Screen in the middle of Woodford Lodge Cricket Grounds, and how we would all be gazing up at it. And how she didn't know what would become of the whole Ragbir family after this. But Papa was quick to shut she down.

"Is something important for Chaguanas!" he growled. "When electricity come, them boys could study in the night, you could read your Bible at any hour. No candles. Me meself, I could work better without straining my eyes in this darkness."

Mammy face look like a mad baker had knead it into folds. Papa left with us. Me in the front with my battery-powered torch in hand, Papa at the tail with a flambeau.

It did feel like the whole of Chaguanas leave they house to come out and see. Everybody waiting impatient in front this flapping silver screen. The Delco generator finally did get crank up and a brilliant white illuminated us all. The title *Fifty Acres* bulleted across the screen. The booming voice of a Yankee accent echo over we heads. We was sitting here in Chaguanas in the late evening and, by some kind of magic, we was watching the sun rising over a homestead in a place called Illinois, in Foreign.

My heart was pounding watching men made into giants by the screen; this was nothing like the small screen in Jubilee. These giants was hoisting electricity poles, tall lamps illuminating the trail from the house to the barn. Huge machines chipping wood, heating up water, streetlights pouring light over the workmen, all marching home at sundown. No burning flambeau over the skin; no torch to suddenly run out of juice.

Then was the glorious scene inside the house. An electric stove. Pots and pans, bubbling and simmering on the top. They had a few things cooking at the same time – hot saucy beans, chicken, steaming white rice.

"Eating everything hot one time," my father murmured to we – neck pushed back, face silver in the light. "Too bad your mother not here. She woulda like that part."

Everybody in the audience did love the indoor four-ring electric stove, until the chef put the spoon in he mouth, and put it right back in the pot. Everybody shout out, *Oh geed! The chef jutaa the pot!*

The final flim was a musical performance by Gogi Grant. Adorned in a silvery threaded dress, her voice echoing the sound of Isaac's favourite song. "The Wayward Wind."

I could see Isaac shelve between my sisters, face long and bright, mouth parted, eyes wide, enraptured. There was a tender feeling about to bloom inside me, something that had the chance to crescendo into brotherly love. He was just a child after all, slipping off somewhere whenever the opportunity presented itself. He disappeared into it – away from us. The tender feeling evaporated as Isaac started staring into the distance. He was staring at Mr Beharry, laughing with a beer in he hand, his thick moustache covered in foam, eyes bloodshot. Isaac was watching round cautiously.

He make a crawl and slip away from we other siblings. I see him exit the field through the small iron gate.

And I had to follow him.

Even though evening was softly passing into night, it still had a heat wafting out from the asphalt under my washikong shoes. The pitch-oil flambeaux lined the road and threw my shadow across the walls of cane lining the Woodford Lodge Factory.

I creep up behind Isaac and wallop a hard one to the back of his head. I pull him by the shoulders, turn him round to face me. "Where the hell you going?"

Isaac wriggled his shoulder free from my fingers. "I wait to see if that bison could call my name."

"Bison? How you mean? Beta?"

Isaac grinned. "Is either Brother Lal gone mad or is Mr Beharry bison he did see that night, standing on two foot, mouth full of gold. I want to see it for mehself!" He push off and start to make for the cemetery. I start running after him.

If we retrospecting, like how I doing now, this boy really choose a good night to make a mischief. Every man jack was gathering in that field, and the whole of Chaguanas Main Road was silent, dead. Only the wicked was out here in this hot night.

I see Isaac, jumping the waterlogged drain, dropping to all fours in the wet grass, creeping behind the headstones, edging around the puddles.

"Ay, ay! Yuh ass! Get back here!" I call out in a harsh whisper.

He laugh and continue to crawl towards the silhouette of the jamun trees, branches long like tendrils, fluttering leaves edging each one. Within the base of the grove, I could see it: a slow heaving, large, black mass blocking the soft glow of the half moon.

I watch Isaac scrape heself across the reddish-brown dirt of the graveyard, so near to the beast. I lunge at him and all I collect in my hand is the warm night air. He roll away from me and into the darkness of the Jamun grove, and all I coulda hear was my own voice asking me, *Why it is I must get blame for this too?*

"Go ahead and kill yuhself, then!" My shout arouse the black mass, and it start to rise up. With a massive tremble of its flesh, it shake off the graveyard dust from the folds of its wrinkled grey skin.

I throw mehself against the gravestone. I could hear the muffled snorting, but it was only when I throw the light of the torch I did see.

Beta there like a behemoth over Isaac, hooves digging rough into the hard earth, horned head tossing rabidly from side to side, thick foam flying out from his mouth.

Isaac's chest was pinned under its front right hoof, his hands around its hock, trying to pull the hoof off. He shouting something, but I was trembling so much, I drop the torch.

The light continue to shine on them as Beta bellowed – loud, deep, the pitch so low, it reverberating in my bones. He lower he muzzle over Isaac, thick white saliva gush into every orifice of Isaac's face, his eyes, nose, his open screaming mouth.

And it was like Jaikaran had said, with the dragging of the tongue – *He Will Laugh* – his once smiling face was being torn into bloody shreds of skin and flesh.

Isaac's scream went higher, like baby now born. No, like a small animal being gutted.

I cover my ears. I cover my eyes. *Not for this too, not for this too,* I was whispering.

The sound of something dragging in the dirt. Then, the splash beyond the jamun grove, beyond the graveyard. The ravine where the bones of old, dead Anglicans longed to push free.

The screaming stop.

I start to run out of the graveyard, slip in a puddle of water, and hit my head on the gravestone of Mr Lowen Bullen.

A faint presence of rain drawing lines down my muddy face when I wake. The earth and my blood congeal over my forehead and my eyes. When I stagger into the main road, I could smell the rain as it beat the warm asphalt, a soft mist curling above it. Through the drizzle, I see a hundred flambeaux coming towards me like a firestorm. Like the whole of Chaguanas looking for we. Within the crowd, I find my father, his face crumpled with the deep exhaustion that only comes when hope is lost at night. Eyes wet, red rims and wide, his mouth too, open wide and a low moan that has no beginning nor end, it goes up and down like the drawn out note of a hymn. But it never end.

"Look he dey!" Is Brother Lal, shouting and pointing.

Mammy push through the crowd, her face like stone. Before words could come out, it was clout after clout. Her hands on my head, my neck, my arms. I let her do it, and I wonder if she will bless me with darkness again, but she suddenly pull back, breathless, sweat leaking down her throat. Somebody holding her back, not my father.

I cough. "We have to go to the graveyard and look for Isaac." My voice cracking, weak. I let myself collapse to the ground, scraping the warm, wet asphalt with my hands. Mammy stare down at me, I could see now it was a church sister holding her. I didn't have no words, it didn't have nothing there.

My mind wasn't working right, but my mouth did start to forge a truth Mammy would listen to. "It was the bison," I say, looking up at the faces crowding over me. "The bison with the mouth full of gold. It was bellowing he name – he Christian name. And ... And he went to it."

Whispers start shooting through the crowd like arrows carrying all my lies so quickly, I coulda never take them back.

"Gabriel, this is what you see?" Her voice was calm.

"And he call heself, 'the Devil's Son,'" I muttered over and over. "He call heself the Devil's Son, he call heself the Devil's Son ..."

The inferno of flambeaux troop through the streets of Chaguanas. Every narrow road, alleyway, drain, no matter how shallow. Where there was darkness, a flaming rag found its way and devoured it. Revealing nothing, no trace, no Isaac.

The rain started pouring harder – reflecting orange against the fire of the flambeaux. A horde of men descend upon the graveyard. I go with them, and Pa remains, the rain mix with his tears. There was a call for more pitch-oil, more rags, more rods. They illuminated the headstones, the red earth of the cemetery. Through the sheets of pouring water, I see the jamun grove, the branches torn away, the hoofprints under it.

Beyond, the thrashing water of the ravine turning wild, flowing away from us, away from me. I watch and wonder if it did channel my sin down to the swamp where it would sleep for all the years to come.

The water around our ankles start to pool and the men cannot resuscitate each flambeau in time as the rain did worsen and storm upon we. The search for Isaac and Beta come to an end.

In the morning, the constable come, and the next day Mammy prepare for a service to be done in Isaac name. Then ten days of nightly prayer for his soul. Prayer to weaken the Devil's hold on my brother. Prayer for some kind of release, some kind of sign.

The rains fall for days, and eventually everybody was ready to give up. Rescue party turn into recovery party to at least find a body.

Papa did continue to search for life. He hold onto me, wild eyes, grip my shoulders, asking: *Did I ever call out Isaac's name while I worked in the cemetery? Was Beta ever looking at Isaac when he walk past? Did I ever hear Beta speak before? Had I ever seen his mouth open wide enough to show teeth glittering like gold?*

Eventually Beta turn up again, once more taking he rightful place under the shade of the swinging jamun branches, consuming all the fallen berries, face still stain bright violet.

Papa took this as his own sign and told Mr Beharry he had to cut Beta open, and there he would find his son in the belly. But Mr Beharry did protest; call police on Papa.

Papa did not leave the house again. Yet did not turn to drink. He stopped working and then find heself in the church.

Then, regular pilgrimage to the Mount, to light a black candle on Mr Beharry head – *Let it fall down dead! Let the beast, the Devil's Son, split open and come bounding out, Isaac!* Papa withers, wails, and I could no longer bring myself to look at him or admire him.

One night, I steal away, like if my name Iscariot, fold myself into the darkness and run deep in the south lands. I become an apprentice of the black gold we call oil and for forty-three years I live in successful amnesia in the heart of Pointe-à-Pierre.

But now in the traffic, the haunting voice of Gogi Grant start to creep up, start to claw up into my own flesh and make me remember everything.

If I return to Chaguanas, would I go in the dry season?

If I look in the bare ravine, would I find him? Would I find Isaac, find him as a boy, never age, standing there whole and complete, laughing back me?

Or would I find him – skin then fascia, nerves and tendon, flesh and fat, then the bare bones – all licked clean by the most corrosive of all elements, the tongue of Beta?

Beta, the one who bellows and vomits fire, eyes bloodshot, this lost bison still looking for its master.

And I, his brother in debauchery, aren't I also the lost son of the Devil's own herd?

I push the power button. I cut Gogi's voice into silence.

The light turns green. The palm of my hand rotates the steering wheel. I guide my car down the San Fernando Bypass, towards my home.

A RIVER THEN
THE ROAD

PIP ROBERTSON

Alexis spotted their dad across the train station car park, and texted their mum. She was allowed a phone once a month, just for these visits.

"Ready?" Alexis said. She took Ben's hand and they ran, hunched over in the rain, dodging puddles to the car.

"I want the blue side!" Ben said. Like always, he insisted on sitting by the mismatched door.

Rain pummelled the roof.

"You look like drowned rats," their dad said.

"Do we have to stay in a motel tonight?" Ben asked.

"Yeah, bit wet for camping." They waited to turn out of the car park, their dad tapping his fingers on the steering wheel in time with the indicator tick. "So, what's new?"

"Not much," said Alexis. She had been invited to Juliet's birthday party, a girl at the centre of a friendship group Alexis had been on the periphery of all year. She had begged her mum to let her go to the party instead, but her mum hadn't wavered. It was their dad's weekend. That was the rule. *There'll be other invites*, she had said, not understanding that turning down an invitation left Alexis in a worse position than not being invited at all.

"I lost another tooth," Ben said, baring his teeth and squishing his tongue in the canine gap.

"Awesome, awesome," their dad said, but he wasn't really listening. He turned the radio on, then off, then on again. He was always nervous at the start.

●　●　●

Their dad had been living with Mick, his old schoolfriend, for two years. For the first year, Alexis and Ben visited their dad there, sleeping in a spare room with creaky beds. Mick had inherited the house from his grandparents, and hadn't changed the furniture. He went to church on Sundays, and seemed like an old person even though he was the same age as their dad. Once Alexis overheard Mick on the phone talking about their dad, saying he was staying while he *battled some demons and found his feet*, and she had imagined him in a cartoonish tumble of monsters and lightsabres.

The last time they'd slept there, Alexis had been in the shower when Mick had come in and stared at her in the mirror while he brushed his teeth. The shower door was glass, and if she tried to cover herself it would have been like accusing him, so she stood still with the water running over her, aware of the scribble of new dark hairs between her legs. When Mick had finished brushing, he wiped his mouth with a wet hand and held a finger to his lips: *shh*. As soon as he left she turned off the water and grabbed her towel. Outside the bathroom were raised voices.

"You alright, Lexi?" her dad had called through the door.

"Yep!" she had yelled back, pulling on her clothes in a rush.

The rest of that day, her dad had kept asking her if she was okay, and she kept saying she was fine. Later, he said, "This morning in the bathroom, Mick just wasn't thinking. It won't happen again. No need to say anything to your mum, eh?"

Alexis didn't need convincing. She hoped no one ever mentioned it again.

They didn't stay at Mick's after that. In bad weather, they went to a motel; in good weather, they went camping – meaning they slept in the station wagon with the seats down flat, in a car park at a forest or beach. Their dad had a little gas stove for instant noodles, and at the supermarket he let them get whatever else they wanted – sweets and chips and sugary drinks, saying that he bet their mum never let them eat that stuff. It was true, she didn't, but Alexis shrugged and said, *sometimes*.

On the camping weekends, even Ben knew better than to tell their mum exactly where they had slept and what they had eaten. On the train home Alexis brushed their hair and made Ben rub toothpaste on his teeth, copying her. For Ben the camping was all still fun, with the boundless choice in the supermarket, not washing, peeing against a tree and sleeping in his clothes. Alexis increasingly dreaded the awkwardness of having nowhere private to get changed, how the car filled up with the smell of their breath, the corrosive feeling in her mouth after all the sugar and salt.

* * *

"You two are like peas in a pod," the motel receptionist said, nodding at Ben and their dad as she handed over the key. It was true – the crooked smile, the curls, but also the way their clothes seemed too big. Their dad was tall, but skinny in a way that looked like he wasn't done growing. Once Ben asked their mum what a *teenager* was. She explained it was someone not quite a child anymore, but not yet a proper adult.

"Like Dad?" Ben had said. Alexis had laughed, but their mum had looked tired.

"No, Ben, your father is an adult."

Alexis knew not to talk about Dad with her anymore, but Ben came back from their visits recounting things their dad had said, not noticing the uncomfortable, careful way Mum responded.

"Dad said he's gonna be his own boss soon."

"Well. Good for him."

"He's gonna organise other people to paint houses so he doesn't have to anymore."

"I hope that works out."

"Then will you get back together? He says you left 'cos he didn't have a good job."

"No, Benny, this is the way things are now."

Alexis never wanted them back together. She was old enough to remember how it had been.

* * *

The rainy day crawled along in the cramped motel room. They borrowed Monopoly from the reception, and Ben insisted on being the banker even though he was slow and got the notes muddled. Their dad started going on about capitalism after landing on Park Lane, which

Alexis owned. The game was abandoned to an argument.

Alexis wondered what everyone was doing at Juliet's. The unfairness of not being there stung.

In the evening, their dad got fish and chips. It was meant to be a treat, but Alexis didn't feel like eating. Ben picked at the chips, his bottom lip protruding, still holding a grudge from Monopoly.

"Eat up, you two," their dad said.

"I'm not really hungry," Alexis said.

"I only like chips with tomato sauce," said Ben. "And this sauce tastes funny."

"It's just different to the one we have at home," Alexis said.

"This *is* your home," their dad said.

"This isn't our home. It's a motel," said Ben, perking up at the opportunity to correct an adult.

"Wrong." Their dad grabbed some chips, stubbed them in the tub of sauce. "You're here with me. So, you're home."

"But we don't have any of our stuff here."

"Stuff isn't important. Doesn't mean anything."

"What about school? We don't go to school here," Ben said.

"None of that matters." Their dad slammed his hand down. "You're *here*, with *me*."

No one said much after that. They watched a movie on the old TV about two bungling police officers. Their dad said it was a classic.

●   ●   ●

Alexis woke to pain in her stomach. The room was dark and still, and she could tell that their dad was out. The pain came and went, a dull stabbing. After a while, headlights glared through the thin curtain, swooped across the wall. Alexis pretended to sleep as he came in with shopping bags and his big backpack. She lay, not moving, and watched him pack it all, then slump, hunched and shaking. *Crying,* Alexis realised with a mixture of thrill and fear. He was *crying*.

He kicked off his shoes and got into bed. The feeling in Alexis's stomach subsided. She tried to stay awake to listen, but if he was crying, it melded with the rattling hum of the mini-fridge, the rain on the roof, the wind.

In the morning, sun slanted in. Their dad was up and dressed, hair wet from a shower, and it was like Alexis had imagined the scene from the night before. They checked out and drove to the beach for a breakfast of chocolate biscuits in the dunes. It was too cold for swimming, but Ben and their dad dug a huge hole and channel to the sea, yelling encouragement at the waves to reach the hole. Alexis drew pictures in the sand with driftwood and signed her name with great, swooping letters. She checked her phone, but there was nothing to see. When her mum had first given her the phone, it had felt, momentarily, like a gate opening onto a new world. But her mum made it clear it was only for emergencies, and only for these visits. She had blocked it from downloading apps, and her mum was the only one with the number. Alexis's argument that other people her age had their own phones hadn't swayed her at all.

Alexis had been given the phone after the visit in March, when their dad hadn't turned up at the station. Trains had rumbled past, and Ben had whined about being hungry and bored. Alexis had been hungry and bored too, but there was no one for her to whine to and nothing to do except sit and wait.

The man from the ticketing window had come over. "You two look like lost luggage," he had said, and lent Alexis his phone. She had tried their dad twice, but he didn't pick up. So she had to call their mum, and because there wasn't a train for two hours, she had driven for an hour to collect them. She had just pulled up, and they were about to get in her car, when their dad arrived. He stopped so his car blocked hers from leaving and got out. Their mum wound down her window.

"No way!" he said. "This is my night."

"Nope. You weren't here, so they're coming home with me."

"A mate was helping me fix my car, it took longer than we thought." His grey car now had a blue door where the dented one had been.

"So what? They're kids! You don't just leave them waiting for hours."

"Chill out, they were fine."

"They were scared." Neither was right.

"One night, Justine. One night a month." Their dad had turned to Alexis and Ben, who were still standing by their mum's car. "You guys wanna come with me, right?"

"You don't have to," their mum said. "You can come home."

Alexis had wished there was a third option, something that would beam her up and away from the car park and this contest between her parents that went on and on, with barbed little victories but never any resolution. Ben tugged at her hand and she let him decide.

"New door!" he said.

"That's right," their dad had said, opening it like a chauffeur, standing wide, waving them in. Alexis had hated his look of triumph.

●　　●　　●

The wind whipped up the sand on the beach, so they walked over the dunes to the playground with the skulking seagulls. Alexis sat on a swing and scuffed her feet. Their dad stood, watching Ben climb up the slide, and Alexis thought he might cry again.

"Can I have a push to get started?" she called out, although she hadn't needed that for years.

He came over and pulled the swing back, making a beeping sound like a reversing truck. As he let go, Alexis dropped her head back and the sky lurched. She moved her legs in and out, swinging until the chains juddered at the top of the arc as if they were trying to buck her off.

On the way to the station, Ben complained that they hadn't had lunch.

"I can't send you back hungry," their dad said, and stopped at the mall. Alexis's stomach felt heavy. She didn't want food, she wanted to be home. This meant they would have to wait until the three o'clock train. At the bakery, their dad filled a bag with cakes and pastries. It was too much, far more than they could eat. Her stomach twisted. That stabbing feeling again.

"I need to go to the toilet," she said.

"Okay, see you back at the car."

Alexis walked through the mall. Her parents had met here, working at shops that didn't exist anymore, her mum an apprentice in the hair salon, her dad at the butcher's, both just out of school, only six years older than Alexis. All her mother ever said about that time was that they had been way too young. In the bathroom, the air thick with pine-scented air freshener not quite masking the other smells, Alexis twisted the lock closed and sat down.

There was a reddish smudge in her pants. She wiped herself, and there were more streaks of red on the paper. It was her first time. She knew what it was – from her mum and from a session at school for which boys had been ushered out of the classroom and the girls were shown diagrams about how to use tampons and pads. Not many girls in her class had had their period yet, or had admitted to having it. They had all been told it was natural and normal and nothing to be ashamed of. But boys playing lunchtime cricket at school had found a tampon once, and took turns throwing the little white bullet at each other, full of derision and disgust. Accusations had circled about whose pocket it had dropped from. Alexis had been mentioned, and like everyone else she had denied it – *no way, as if* – but she felt tainted all the same.

She folded toilet paper into a wad and put it in her pants, hoping it would last the couple of hours until she was home.

Leaving the bathroom, she was sure people were staring. *Can everybody see?* A group of teenagers erupted into laughter as she passed and her face burned, thinking the blood must be showing. But she glanced sideways: they were in a huddle, fixated on one of their phones.

Ben and her dad were waiting in the car.

"You were ages," Ben said, with a mouthful of cake.

Their dad said they had time to kill and drove in the opposite direction to the train station. The town wasn't big. Within a few streets, houses became sparse; then they were driving past farmland, cows and sheep and mathematical rows of something green. Their dad had started doing that thing where he talked on and on, looking at them in the rear-view mirror.

"The thing is, the system gears us to be dissatisfied with what we have. It's like sugar. They load it into everything – bread, mayonnaise, you name it. So basically, we're all addicted. We crave it, but we need more and more of it to actually taste sweetness. Go back and measures of status were different. Cars? Didn't exist. En-suites? There wasn't indoor plumbing! A few hundred years ago, if you got to my age with your own teeth in your head, you were winning."

Ben didn't even pretend to listen. He dabbed his finger against his tongue and made a pattern on the car window with his spit. Alexis just wanted their dad to keep his eyes on the road as it got steeper, winding. She guessed he was taking them to a forest park where they had camped a couple of times. Alexis didn't like staying there. Even on nice days, it felt gloomy, closed in by trees and mountains, and it was popular with hunters, who frightened Alexis with their guns strapped to their backs and their bristling, impatient dogs. Now their dad was talking about food productivity. The toilet paper between her legs was bunched up and uncomfortable. They drove past the entrance to the car park where they had stayed, and then turned off down a narrow, unsealed road with bush pressing in each side. They needed to turn around now if they had any hope of making the three o'clock train.

"Dad? Shouldn't we be heading back?" she said.

"There's no reason for anyone to be going hungry."

"Dad?"

"There are *four hundred* golf courses in New Zealand alone. Four hundred!" A few minutes later he came to a stop, motor still running. "Out we get."

Alexis and Ben stood at the side of the road. He opened the boot and unpacked their bags.

"What about the train?" Alexis said, but he was back in the car, wheels spinning on stones, and then he was gone. The sound of the car faded, and the silence left behind was too big.

"Is he coming back?" Ben whispered.

Alexis had no idea. "Yeah, of course," she said, like he was dumb for asking.

"What if he doesn't? I'm hungry."

"Eat, then." Alexis nudged the bag at their feet, from the bakery. "God, don't be such a baby," she said, trying to keep her own worry in check, sick of having to be the one to reassure.

She got the phone out of her backpack. There was no reception. Ben sat down, eating a donut quickly and unhappily. The sun dipped behind the trees and the drop in temperature was immediate.

"Jacket on," she said, making her voice soft. Ben hated his jacket because it was yellow, and used to be Alexis's and still had her name written inside. But when she held it out he put it on without complaining. She wiped cream from the corner of his mouth and handed him a chocolate milk. She was going to take one too, but worried that drinking would make more blood come. "Dad'll be back real soon, Benny. Any minute." As if on cue, their dad jogged into view.

"Man, you should see your worried faces!" he laughed and stood, hands on hips, catching his breath. "Good news! It's camping time. I spoke to your mum earlier and she agreed you can stay another night."

"Where's the car?" Alexis asked.

"I had to find a spot for it. There's no room to park here."

"Where are we going to sleep?"

He gestured at the forest behind her. "In there." She hadn't noticed the start of a track. "We're going to do proper camping. I've got a new tent." He hoisted on his backpack, so bulky that he almost lost his balance. "Ready for an adventure?"

He started walking. Ben shouldered his own bag and scrambled after him, and all Alexis could do was follow. The track was overgrown, or maybe it had never been well-formed. Orange tags nailed onto trees marked the route. Leaves held onto yesterday's rain and dampened her clothes as she passed. Mud sucked at her sneakers. Had their mum really said they could stay? They had missed a visit two months earlier when she and Ben were sick. It was possible she'd agreed to make up for that. But with school the next day? And there was the other problem ... Alexis slowed down, slipped her hand down the front of her jeans and touched her underpants. Her fingers came back red. She called out that she needed to go to the toilet.

"We'll wait," her dad called back.

She found a spot hidden by bushes and pulled down her jeans. The toilet paper was sodden and shocking red. She scuffed a hole in the earth with her heel, dropped the wad in and covered it. Blood was showing through on the outside of her jeans. She opened her bag trying to find something to use, but they never brought much with them. It was only meant to be one night.

"You okay, Lexi?" her dad called out, and she could see him through the trees, coming towards her. She grabbed a sock and stuffed it in her underpants.

"Coming," she called back, pulling up her jeans. She took off her jacket and tied it around her waist.

She thought about telling him. Maybe he would say they could go back. But did men even know about it? What if he didn't understand, or didn't believe her? What if he wanted to see?

"Here, have some water. This walking is thirsty work." He handed her a bottle. She took it and pretended to drink.

* * *

They perched on a log, eating instant noodles. Alexis was relieved it was nearly dark. She couldn't see the state of her jeans, which meant neither could Ben or her dad. Alexis only ate the noodles, tilting her bowl and pouring out the liquid when they weren't looking. Their dad packed away the gas cooker and said it was time to go.

"We're not staying here?" she said.

"We'd roll down the hill in our sleep. We'll be on flat ground soon."

"But it's dark," Ben said.

"Good thing I thought ahead." Their dad rummaged in a pocket of his backpack then dangled a headlamp in front of each of them. "Told you this would be an adventure."

He helped adjust the elastics, showed them where the ON buttons were, and they set off again. Three bright eyes in the night.

* * *

Alexis stared at the blank blue of the tent wall. She had *almost* believed their mum had agreed to an extra night. But in the lamplight the previous night, when her dad was getting the tent out of his pack, she'd seen a big bag of rice, packets of noodles, extra gas canisters ... enough for days and days, far more days than their mum would ever agree to. She could see now it was all deliberate, walking on this track that didn't even have a sign, the car parked who knows where. He didn't want them to be found. But the longer it went on, the more trouble he would be in – and not just from their mum.

She rolled over carefully. Ben was a scruff of hair at the top of the sleeping bag next to her, and her dad was a featureless mound on the other side. She gathered her things and eased up the tent zip, glad that sleeping through anything was another way in which her dad and brother were the same.

Outside it was light, but not fully, like the colour of the world was still getting turned up.

Everything was covered by a soft fuzz of moss, and beech trees stretched up towards the brightening sky. Walking at night, it had seemed the trees were props that sprung up when she shone her light on them and collapsed when they were in the dark again. Now she could see the trees went on forever.

Alexis moved away from the tent and squatted down, but no wee came out. The sock had moved out of place in her sleep, and her underpants and jeans were a mess. She smelled bad down there. Not drinking was working though, she noted with relief. The blood was coming out thicker and darker, like it was drying up. It was worth feeling thirsty.

She needed to start walking.

The day before they had walked for five hours, maybe six. Her phone had run out of battery and her had dad said the time didn't matter. If she left now she could maybe contact her mum by lunchtime; they could be home in the afternoon, and sleep in their own beds that night. Maybe it could all be explained as a misunderstanding.

There was the matter of her jeans. She needed to find a river or a stream to wash herself. They hadn't crossed any on the track walking in, but she thought she had heard water a few times. Then, when she was clean, she would find the road and walk until she saw people and could ask to call her mum. *A river then the road,* she repeated in her head. She found an orange track marker nailed to a tree and started to walk.

●   ●   ●

Water. She was sure of it. She turned sideways to edge down the slope, using trees as handrails to steady herself. But where it seemed there should be water, there was only the sound of it, and more forest, more slope. She kept going down until she reached the bottom of a gully. There might have been a river there once, but she had heard only the ghost of it, or a trick of the wind, because there was no water there now. She had wasted what, an hour? She started climbing. It was slower and harder, pulling herself up. When she thought she had climbed enough, she looked for a marker on a tree – but there were none. The forest made false paths, with tree roots suggesting stairs, ferns seeming to line a trail, before ending in a rock or a drop or a dense tangle of bush.

Her tongue felt like carpet, throat like sand. She would give anything for a drink. It had been dumb not to take any food from the tent. She sat down and looked through her bag, just in case. Toothpaste? She squeezed the tube into her mouth, thinking it might at least get rid of the rough feeling, but the gob of gel was thick and gummy. She didn't have enough saliva to spit it out, so had to wipe her tongue on her sleeve.

The sun was beyond its high point, so it must be afternoon. It had been in front of them yesterday, so if she kept it behind her, surely she would reach a road eventually. She made herself stand, made herself keep going.

The sun tracked its way across the sky. *Had anyone walked here, ever?*

The trees thinned and she hoped, briefly, that she was coming to the edge of the forest. She imagined emerging into a backyard with white sheets flapping on a washing line. But no. She stood on a rocky ledge, and the ground dropped away and a valley spread out before her. There were mountains waiting behind the mountains. The low sun caught on the seam of water far below, turning the surface gold. She had found her river, but it was impossible to reach.

Wind blew and she could see its progress, a huge invisible hand skimming across the trees like velvet pushed the wrong way.

It would be cold soon. Everything ached. Pain knuckled her head. Her tongue was too big for her mouth. Her body was a too-heavy thing she was sick of hauling around. Time to rest.

Back in the forest, Alexis found a hollow in the earth beside a fallen beech tree. It would fit her fine. She lay on her side, the way she always fell asleep. She pulled her green jacket around her. The ferns formed an awning, and the tree was reassuring against her back. Nothing here minded the blood. The smell of her was just another smell alongside sap and damp earth and rotting wood. She was lost luggage. Her mum would come and get her, or her dad would find her. Next to her face, her hand was resting on fallen beech leaves, each the size of a fingernail and coloured dark green, or red, or brown, the same shade as her hair. Alexis shut her eyes.

● ● ●

The white dog moves through the night forest, a whorl of muscle and intention. Time is running out. His people are tired. He absorbs the scents from the earth, the scents in the air, his whole being filtering them.

Then – there – a scent, pulling him along a ridge, over rocks, moss, through the bush. There is nothing elective to this movement. The scent splits, intensifies, and he slows, nose to the ground. He is close. *Tree ... tree ... tree ... ferns ... girl.*

She is oil and salt and a streak of chemical mint and blood. Most of all, she is blood. Wounded? He nudges at her. Not wound blood, but her own, old, and new.

The girl jerks and opens her eyes. Fear rises off her like steam. He inhales it, and the hairs on his neck stiffen automatically, his mouth ready to snarl. But she doesn't move, just lies, body tense, breath like she has been running. Then, because he has been so long, two faint whistle blasts. He tilts his head towards the sound, then back to consider her. He whines. He could bark. He could draw his people here.

No. She is not the animal they need.

And he is off, running again through the scents, trying to find a good one before the night is done.

AUTHOR AND TRANSLATOR BIOGRAPHIES

Sanjana Thakur
OVERALL WINNER
AND REGIONAL WINNER: ASIA

Sanjana Thakur is a writer from Mumbai, India. She is the 2024 winner of the *Pigeon Pages* poetry contest, and was a finalist for the 2024 Jesmyn Ward Fiction Prize. Her fiction has appeared or is forthcoming in *Granta*, *The Rumpus* and *The Southampton Review*. Her poetry has been supported by the Bread Loaf Environmental Writers' Conference, and is forthcoming in *Pigeon Pages* and *Booth Magazine*. She is a graduate of UT Austin's New Writers Project and Wellesley College. She is currently at work on a short-story collection.

Reena Usha Rungoo

REGIONAL WINNER: AFRICA

Reena Usha Rungoo is a Mauritian writer, scholar, teacher, speaker and mother. As an islander, an African and a diasporic South Asian, she uses the language of fiction (whether as a writer or a literary critic) to speak on how colonial violence infiltrates our beings, our languages and our desires, and on the creative ways in which we resist. She is an assistant professor of literature at Harvard University.

Julie Bouchard

REGIONAL WINNER: CANADA AND EUROPE

Julie Bouchard is a native and resident of Montréal, and has released two collections of short stories and a novel over the last decade with La Pleine Lune, a Québec-based publishing house. She was awarded the Radio-Canada Short Story Prize in both 2020 and 2021. She currently works in academic publishing.

Arielle Aaronson is a translator from French to English of novels, films and more. Her translation of Marie-Renée Lavoie's *Autopsy of a Boring Wife* was longlisted for the 2021 *Canada Reads* competition, and her translation of Paul Tom's *Alone* was shortlisted for the 2023 Governor General's Literary Award. She lives in Montréal with her family.

Portia Subran
REGIONAL WINNER: THE CARIBBEAN

Portia Subran is a writer and ink artist from Chaguanas, Trinidad and Tobago. Her stories are inspired by her parents' tales of colonial and early postcolonial Trinidad, lived experience and ole talk gathered over the years. She is the winner of the 2019 Cecile de Jongh Literary Prize from *The Caribbean Writer* (University of the Virgin Islands) for her short story "Twice the World", and the 2016 Small Axe Literary Short Story Competition for "Mango Feast". She has been published in *Pree Lit Magazine* and *The Caribbean Writer*.

Pip Robertson

REGIONAL WINNER: THE PACIFIC

Pip Robertson has had short stories published in journals and anthologies in print and online. She has an MA from the International Institute of Modern Letters at Te Herenga Waka – Victoria University of Wellington. She lives in Te Whanganui-a-Tara, Aotearoa New Zealand, with her partner, daughter and dogs.

Selected Titles from Paper + Ink

www.paperand.ink